Maria

MARGARET HASWELL

PENTLAND PRESS, INC.
UNITED STATES OF AMERICA

PUBLISHED BY THE PENTLAND PRESS, INC.
5124 Bur Oak Circle, Raleigh, North Carolina 27612
United States of America
919-782-0281

ISBN 1-57197-004-5
Library of Congress Catalog Card Number: 95-68517

Printed in the United States of America

For Shirley, of course

AUTHOR'S NOTE

Christopher J Roberts Photography

Much has been written about the American Civil War, a favorite theme for both the novelist and the historian. In this story, however, I have chosen to unravel some of the skeins of that earlier war of a nation struggling to break from the shackles of its colonial past. While I have tried to be historically accurate, I have also used artistic license.

This story is a fictional interpretation of Maria Alston's life. Maria was born in the South Carolina low country during the protracted American War of Independence. She was born into a family of planters and patriots. Their lives were entwined with the politics of the nation at that time, but they were equally interwoven around the demands of the rice culture. The cycle of the rice harvesting affected their daily lives. Rice became of such importance that it was not only exported to European markets in huge quantities, but the staple was also used for money, even in payment of taxes.

Maria, the daughter of a fabulously wealthy rice planter, refused to be ruled by the wishes of her dynastic plantation family. She abandoned the South Carolina low country to "tread the boards" on the New York stage. Through her tangled relationships with her family, friends, and lovers the turbulent political and theatrical events of late eighteenth century America are played out.

The story of the Alston family is one of particular interest to me because I am a descendent of Maria's sister, Charlotte Alston Wilson. After learning of my roots in Pawleys Island, South Carolina, I began the research that became the basis for this book. The Oaks, the original Alston estate, is where my ancestors are buried. I became fascinated with the tragic lives and exciting times of this family. It was from this fascination and research that *Maria* was born.

Margaret Haswell

ACKNOWLEDGMENTS

I gratefully acknowledge the assistance I have been given in gaining access to collections in the archives of the South Carolina Historical Society in Charleston, and Rhodes House Library in the University of Oxford. I am indebted to many kind friends, especially those in Charleston, Georgetown, and on the Waccamaw, and I particularly wish to thank Tom and Carol Pinckney for all their help.

Chapter One

No one could forget the scandal over Grandpa Joseph's will. When Grandpa Joseph's father died of cholera at only forty-four, a thousand acres of cleared jungle lay back from Waccamaw; but it was Grandpa Joseph who built The Oaks from massive hewn timbers.

Maria was six years old when Grandpa Joseph died in the east wing; and she had cried because she loved him. Of course, she did not know of Grandpa Joseph's roll of patriot rebels ready to fight when the Revolution came. She did not know that Grandpa Joseph had another secret roll—a roll of Loyalists to the British Crown to be exposed when the Revolution came. What she remembered was Grandpa with the plantation smiths forging weapons, exhorting her small brother Joseph to keep away from the anvil. She remembered Mama making cornbread for Papa's guerrillas who joined General "Swamp Fox" Marion's patriot forces that harried the British Army up and down Waccamaw's watercourses.

Grandpa Joseph called Maria and her brother his "little freedom fighters" although the Declaration of Independence had been signed two years before Maria was born. But Grandpa Joseph said that was just the beginning.

• • • • •

When it came to the great ballroom, William Alston had decided on a twin staircase sweeping up to the landing from the back of the room. He had built his fine, two-story mansion on a high bluff in full view of his vast swamp lands and had called it "Clifton". Since the day he moved his family to their new home, The Oaks stood empty. It was on that day for the first time that Maria heard what she would many times recall. Her father had looked back as they left The Oaks and had shouted "Our ancestral home, to miss a generation and go to a mere child—it's an outrage!"

Resting her chin in cupped hands Maria leaned her elbows on the dressing table and faced herself in the mirror. "Poor Joseph," she thought. She picked up a brush and slowly passed it through her thick black hair catching the likeness to her father. She had the same compelling eyes with dilating pupils that sometimes struck fear in others, the same long aquiline nose giving an air of hauteur, and the same capricious mouth with a tendency to curl at the left-hand corner in faint amusement. In the mirror, she watched her maid lay out her ballgown. "No more finishing school," she told herself lightheartedly. "No more scolding for running wild in the scorching sun without her wide-brimmed hat." Sometimes she thought she should have been a boy. But today, as debutante of the year, she knew hearts would beat for her. However, it was Joseph's approval she wanted. Her adored brother had not been home for months. It was all the fault of Grandpa Joseph's will. He had left The Oaks to Joseph, insulting Papa with the gift of Fairfield when naturally he had expected to inherit The Oaks. Since then, Joseph had never seemed to please Papa.

Maria thought back with longing to their early morning gallops together before Joseph entered Princeton College. They had shared secrets—Joseph's enthusiasm for politics, her ambition to become an actress.

◆ ◆ ◆ ◆ ◆

Maria's coming out ball was an occasion which brought to William Alston's mind his and his family's move to Clifton. That first night, Mary, his first wife, lying in his arms in the new mahogany four-poster bedstead, which he had had elaborately carved with sheaves of rice, had whispered, "Home darling!" Casting his eyes round the great hall, which was made ready for Maria's coming out ball, he called back the past. He remembered Mary's lips pressed on his, the ecstasy of rediscovery in a long caress, the sweet agony of their love making after years of continual partings. And then, there had been the stupendous housewarming party they gave. The smokehouse had been filled with cured hams. There was a galantine of calf's head garnished with sweetbreads and truffles, along with roast duck, and southern spoonbread. What a cruel fate that their newfound happiness so tragically ended at the birth of their baby daughter Charlotte.

He was thinking how proud Mary would have been when the president, during his tour of South Carolina, had decided to stay at Clifton and had personally thanked every patriot planter on Waccamaw Neck for his heroic part in the Revolution. Maria had been a gangling thirteen year old at the time. He called to mind how she had dramatically appeared on the piazza like some prima donna, dressed in a long white muslin frock with a band on her forehead with the words "Hail to the Chief" sewn in huge letters. What a stir it had caused. He sought to marry Maria into one of the leading planter families. He had invited to her coming-out ball all who had been his house guests when President George Washington had visited, but tonight they would be accompanied by their sons and daughters. He was thinking one of the Haggar boys would make an admirable son-in-law, when he was joined by his second wife, Motte. He refused to call her by any other name, for she too, was a Mary.

Motte, who was nearer in age to Maria, was just twenty-two when William carried her off to Clifton to become the new plantation mistress. Cut off from her comfortable Charleston upbringing she had to learn to survive in the sweltering Waccamaw temperatures, which never fell below the eighties and were always accompanied by the high humidity which bears upon the air the dreaded rice fevers. When William had spoken of the Clifton ménage, with so many household slaves to contend with, she had panicked. Horribly jealous, her two lively sisters had laughed to scorn that she had been chosen before them to be the consort of so distinguished a gentleman.

"Why, your nose is too large," they had scoffed. "Either of us would make a prettier colonel's lady!" But Motte's mother, herself a doubly-honored patriot for acts of bravery during the Revolution, had welcomed the union of their two great houses.

As she crossed the ballroom to speak to her husband, Motte stopped and absently rearranged a spray of coral vine, the heart-shaped leaves giving it the name "love-chain". She was hoping a suitor could be found for Maria. The girl still made her feel like an intruder in her own house. To William she said, "I do not think the smallest detail has been overlooked."

William's piercing look had a hint of amusement. He liked his wife's chubby face. Her wide-set eyes gave the impression of childlike innocence, though she had borne three times in the space of three years. "I can find no fault with the décor," he said, as he swung hawkish, hooded eyes into every corner of the ballroom. "And you, my dear," he said as he studied her upturned face above a short neck and a plump little figure, "you look just dandy." He was in a receptive mood. Everything boded well. He leaned with his six foot six frame, and tweaked her nose.

• • • • •

For the first time in his life, Joseph felt liberated. Stimulated by the post-Revolutionary aspirations of his fellow college students, he had thrown himself into the political arena, a hotbed of ideological clashes. New young blood was reacting against pre-Revolutionary hard-liners. These young men were swift to court slander, abuse, and vituperation. On one occasion, they involved themselves in a personal encounter with pistols at ten paces.

Joseph had entered Princeton College a shy, inarticulate, private person. He was an unprepossessing youth of medium height, with heavy jowls, dark hair and thick build. Often, he wished Grandpa Joseph had not left him The Oaks, making him the object of his father's contempt, to be castigated unworthy of the inheritance. Often Joseph thought Grandpa Joseph would turn in his grave if he knew father had refused to reside at the mansion, even for the few years remaining before he came into full possession under the terms of Grandpa Joseph's will. Of course, his entitlement to the income from the lucrative acres of rice, left in the care of an overseer, made Joseph a very wealthy young man. But the mansion was fast decaying. Vines covered the outside walls. It may never see the lights up again. Joseph thought it symbolic of everything in his past he wanted to discard.

If Maria hadn't insisted on her favorite brother attending her coming out ball, he would not be riding the jungle-cleared highway now, having picked up a fresh horse at the last staging post on his journey south. He would have instead turned north the short distance from Princeton to New York, to take part with his friends in a political rally. Lately, he and his friends had become hypnotized by the brilliant orator and political renegade, Aaron Burr, a regular guest speaker, and one-time graduate of the college, who filled them with wild enthusiasm.

Joseph had grown a beard which marked a change in character.

◆ ◆ ◆ ◆ ◆

Long before the time set for the ball, fiddlers were tuning up on the sunny verandah. Maria had indelicately run to the front portico in her expansive organdy ballgown, to listen for the sound of a galloping horse which she knew would be Joseph's. Her heart, beneath the trim-chested bosom, beat with the same passion she had put into an amateur play in Charleston when she had masqueraded as a flirt whose head ran so upon beaux. That had been acting; this, however, filled her with an agony of apprehension. She needed Joseph's support. She had to talk to Papa tonight.

But instead, charmingly appareled ladies accompanied by gentlemen of large fortune—half the planter fraternity on the Neck who never missed a ball—and curtsying debutantes discreetly searching for a favorite beau from beneath lowered eyes, were graciously being received in a slow-moving procession; while Negro servants cooled the air with large peacock fans. Still, there was no sign of Joseph.

Danny Haggar could not take his eyes off Maria. He thought her the most beautiful girl on Waccamaw and he spent the best part of the evening trying to catch her fiery black eyes. At last, this dance would be his.

"Miss Alston, Maria, would you...?" Maria had turned her head to overhear a group of arguing gentlemen.

"Sshush? They're talking about the Pawley boys. Never been forgiven for having a Loyalist father. Seems they're putting their plantation on the market. Guess your father and mine are in a neck and neck fight for it!"

Danny said, "My Pa has promised me a plantation when I marry." He flushed to the roots of his hair as Maria gave him a quizzical look. He nerved himself to take her hand. Passion flooded from his fingertips, but she saw only the callow youth who had been her childhood playmate. She had no intention of becoming a bargaining chip for a plantation.

"Anyway," she said in a clear voice, "I feel sorry for those Pawley boys. They don't stand a chance."

The knot of arguing planters turned with black looks. Danny gave a gasp of horror. What he wanted to say, suddenly he couldn't say. The band struck up for the next dance, and another suitor claimed Maria.

• • • • •

A family row in public was beneath William Alston's dignity. He had been born into an elitist society in a southern slave state during the stormy years before the Revolution. Schooled in the philosophies at the best Charleston houses, he had been taught at an early age to savor the fine French wines smuggled into Charleston harbor that graced the lavish tables of Charleston's upper-crust. But, his abiding passions had been vacationing at The Oaks plantation with its endless carpet of exotic green-gold ripening rice stirring his imagination, going on wild duck shoots, and exploring the forest on the back of an Indian pony.

Everything around him at The Oaks he knew would one day be his: the house slaves, the field gangs, the lands, the alligator-infested streams, the Waccamaw swamps. The shock had been devastating when he learned that his father had bypassed him and had instead left him Fairfield, the land and Negro slaves of a run-down plantation he had purchased years back from his old friend Haggar. William had spurned the gift and set out to build his own place with that Huguenot toughness he had inherited from his maternal grandmother and Alston spirit he had inherited from his paternal grandfather. Whether it was the huge breakfast of seafood and game, supported by a selection of his finest French wines, that had prompted George Washington's remarks when he visited Clifton he could not tell, but the president had exclaimed, "Never would I have dreamt of discovering so fairy-like a vista, thousands of acres of well-regulated rice fields interspersed between Waccamaw and Peedee Rivers."

The Haggars were not just close friends and neighbors, they were also staunch patriots. As soon as the last guests had driven away, William faced his two eldest children and gave vent to his anger. "You disgraced me tonight," he started with Maria.

Maria had felt his wrath in that cold expression she knew well; she knew there was no escaping it however long the evening. Was it because she had spoken up for the Pawley boys, or because she had jilted Danny Haggar, she wondered. "I am sorry if I have offended you Papa," she said.

"You know perfectly well every patriot wants Pawley off the Neck," he said. "Your remarks were most distasteful."

"But sir, they are nothing," Joseph intervened. "Reckless youths squandering their fortune. Couldn't care a button how it was gotten."

William turned with his eyes blazing. "And you! How dare you arrive to meet our guests not attired as a gentleman, in travel stained riding breeches and unshaven. One dear lady almost fainted, thought you a brigand! Caused me grave embarrassment!"

A brigand! Maria wanted to laugh. But her father was speaking to her again. "No lady must be left unattached. I noticed you with young Haggar. I have given much thought to your future, and I strongly favor a union between our two families. It is my intention to return Fairfield to the Haggar estate as part of your dowry."

A blind fury seized Maria. "And it is my intention to remain unattached," she said. "I am going to be an actress!"

Her outburst left William momentarily speechless, and Joseph seized the moment to make his own confession. "And I intend to go into politics!"

"My daughter! Tread the boards! Exhibit herself on the stage! It is unthinkable!" William said, ignoring Joseph's confession.

"Charleston is famed for music and drama," Maria said. "I shall lodge with Aunt Polly. Nothing will deter me." Maria gathered up the folds of her ballgown and rushed from the room closing her ears.

"I will not be persuaded," William called after her. "And you," he turned to Joseph as the door slammed behind them, "it is high time you took up your rightful place as a planter. The shame of it is I was too long away fighting when you and Maria were young. Grandpa Joseph has left a devil in you both!"

"You forget, sir, I am of independent means," Joseph shot back as he too moved to leave the room. He paused, on a thought, to cast a last taunt over his shoulder, "Do you know what the Waccamaw planters call you? King Billy! And they do not mean it kindly!"

Chapter Two

A long low whistle woke Maria with a start. She leapt from bed and flung open the shutters. It was the witching hour; sorcery was in the eerie cry of the night owl. Joseph put a warning finger to his lips.

"Wait for me!" she mouthed thinking him calling her for a starlit gallop.

Joseph shook his head vigorously.

"You're not leaving?" she said grimacing as it dawned on her.

His stage whisper floated up to her, "Don't worry. I'll be back." He blew her a kiss, wrapped his dark cloak closer about him, and reined his horse toward the swamplands bordering the Waccamaw River. But she was not deceived for he was riding Touppa, his own beloved stallion. He had not taken Touppa with him previously. She snapped the shutters together angrily. Why did he have to leave? He could have waited.

She was still standing by the shutters when the kitchen servants began thump, thump, thumping on the flagstones outside, pounding unhusked rice in wooden mortars for the day's needs. She thought her head would burst. She wanted to scream. Soon the entire household would be noisily scurrying about, infants squalling, no privacy anywhere, not even in her own room with Charlotte continually coming in to talk to her big sister. And in-between times her maid would be fussing about. Already she felt stifled, and yet the sun had not yet risen. Flinging on some clothes she slipped out of the house before she was missed at the breakfast table.

• • • • •

Mauma, who had been with the family from the day the "Maussa" married the first Mrs. Alston, said repeatedly, "That missy Maria always know what she want and she gits what she want." But Mauma would not have been nursemaid to any other if the choice had been hers. The child had warmth beneath that wild exterior which radiated happiness.

But today, the storm clouds were deeply drawn across Maria's brow. "Marry Danny Haggar? I shall marry whom I please!" were her violent thoughts behind the angry stride. Since the plantation house was on a high bluff, the path she took was downhill. Below, the vast swamplands were still hidden by heavy mists after the fall in night temperatures. She passed the "street" of Negro cabins, deaf to the women's early morning Gullah jabber and barn hens clucking, when she came to a log, a discarded end left by one of the Negro carpenters. She sat down with a glorious feeling of freedom.

Her thoughts drifted to her dream world. Charleston had just completed rebuilding its famous theatre on Dock Street when she reached finishing school. It had been left a heap of rubble after a fire during the Revolution, and for years was forgotten. She remembered the thrill of that first school outing to see Mercy Warren's tragedy in five acts, and the hilarity when gallery hoodlums had hurled missiles into the orchestra. Afterward, she got the lead in the school play, a melodrama espousing the patriot cause, and the Dock Street Theatre's actor-manager had been invited to a gala performance at the school. She had blushed with excitement when he had praised her acting and had said she had real talent.

So engrossed was she in her fantasies that she did not notice the mists lift off the swamplands, the pale dawn light pick out stagnant pools, silent breeding grounds for fever-carrying mosquitoes. Negro field gangs fanned out across the rice plats and began checking banks and ditches for alligator damage. Trunk-minders checked the sluice-gates hewn from live oaks with two facing doors, set at intervals in the huge earth banks to control the inflow and outflow of water irrigating the young shoots.

No one heard Maria's sudden scream or saw her spring up. She had disturbed a colony of giant ants, and the sight of them turned her stomach. Deflated, she hurried back to the house, remembering a too horrible story of a man eaten to the bone by ants as he lay wounded and alone in the forest.

◆ ◆ ◆ ◆ ◆

Coal black Mauma said, "De Maussa, he bin lookin' for yo. What you bin a-doin' gul?"

Maria had never known a time without Mauma. Mauma ran the nursemaids and she had the affection of all the children. "Only went for a walk," she said lamely.

"Best git out o' dem clothes and freshen yoursel' before yo Pa sets eyes on yo," she said as an infant squalled and she waddled off with a disapproving headshake.

"I'll wear a hoop and layers of chiffon," Maria called after her defiantly. She soaked in a tub of warm water. She wanted to impress her father and stop being treated like a schoolgirl. She thought she'd go mad if he didn't let her take the drama course. "He was always in a better mood when he had had a lime punch," she thought. She would be awfully apologetic and would beg him to let her go to Charleston. She became impatient for him to return from overseeing his vast domains.

The plantation house buzzed with life, but she could not settle herself. To take the buggy out in the midday sun to visit the Haggar boys for a gossip would be too exhausting. She went to the library to find a book, forgetting John Ashe and William Algernon were at their lessons.

"Why Miss Alston," their tutor said surprised.

"Oh my!" Maria began to withdraw.

"Please don't go," he said hastily. "Lessons are almost finished for today."

"Thanks, sis," Algernon grimaced as he and John Ashe made their escape.

"Cheeky devil," Maria threw after him. Alone with the bashful twenty-year-old tutor, she said, "I shall call you Piers. You may call me Maria." She was thinking, he was real smart looking, not bullish and red-necked like the horse-racing, duck-shooting boys around here. She looked straight into his soulful blue eyes. "How do you find our southern ways?"

"Real good. It's beautiful country. I'm a nature lover and I write verses," he said blushing fiercely. "Every morning I listen to the plaintive call of the curlews on the creeks, and the hissing cicadas under my window. They are like an invisible orchestra." Waccamaw planters had been surprised at William Alston's choice of a tutor for his sons from far north Connecticut, where New Englanders called Yankees lived with a history of witch-hunting and persecuting people for their faith. But William Alston had answered that he had done it for the Connecticut troops, heroes of the Bunker Hill slaughter when other colonists sided with the English forces; and he respected their scholastic reputation.

"But what about the mosquitoes?" Maria pressed. "Don't you worry about swamp fever, cholera? Doesn't the heat, the awful stickiness, make you feel wretched?"

"In my hometown the winters are cruel cold," he said.

"I hate this place!" Maria said glaring at the shuttered windows. "It's suffocating." She turned and the fiery assault stirred in him an earthy passion. "I came looking for a play," she said moving over to the shelves. "Papa has nothing but treatises on the Revolution."

"I have a book of poems," Piers said hopefully, "and a few verses of my own." He flushed.

"No plays? I'm anxious to read *The Prince of Parthia*," she said. "There's been so much talk about it."

"Matter of fact, I saw it in New York," Piers said. "It wasn't well acted, and the story line is dull—ghosts of dead kings, beautiful women who take poison."

"But have you got it? she said. "After all, it is the first play to be written by an American. It's scandalous not to support our own."

He felt impotent. She didn't want to read his verses. Getting a copy of the play became an obsession.

•   •   •   •   •

Homer, in Alston red and green livery edged with silver piping, his scrubbed black face a shining mask, brought a tray of refreshing lime punch to the piazza. William Alston reached for a glass without looking his way, and stared, entranced at the vast carpet of rice paddy fields. It had been a good day. He'd bought Weehawka. He was thinking old George Pawley would turn in his grave, the Loyalist traitor.

Motte had only a mild cordial in her hand, being again with child. She did not share her husband's elation. George Pawley's grandchildren had been good neighbors, especially Hannah. The ladies circle still relived Hannah's marriage to young Norris. It had been quite the event of the season on Waccamaw. Hannah had looked radiant in a fine India muslin trimmed with handsome lace and a becoming headdress of two ostrich feathers. But oh, the wedding breakfast! Nothing was forgotten. The preserve of fowl—a dove into a quail, the quail into a guinea hen, the guinea hen into a wild duck, the duck into a capon, the capon into a goose, finally the goose into a peacock, each bird well basted and seasoned before being inserted, white and dark meat placed alternately. And the crowning success was the drink with the bridecake. Motte was thinking she would miss them. There was a bit of life about them. So engrossed was she in thought that she had not noticed Maria join them till William broke the spell with a call for another lime punch.

"Here, Papa," Maria took the punch from Homer and handed it to him herself.

William's mood instantly changed. "You were not at breakfast," he said. "What explanation have you?"

"None really, Papa. I'm sorry. But please, let me go to drama school," she blurted out.

"Absolutely no," he said. "I will not have you tread the boards. It is the first duty of a girl to marry. In the future you will accompany Motte on her daily rounds, learn the art of a good plantation mistress because that's what you are going to be very shortly."

"Maria!" Motte shrieked as the girl lammed out at her father striking him blow after blow on the chest. But Motte's pleas for sanity were drowned, and all she had was a vision of a cockfight, with tearing claws and flying feathers.

◆ ◆ ◆ ◆ ◆

Motte took her place at the long refectory table opposite her husband. Her infant children were already tucked in their beds by their nursemaids. Her stepchildren took their seats on either side, Maria, John Ashe, Algie and little Charlotte. One place remained unoccupied. No one spoke of Joseph's absence. No one spoke at all of anything that might send Papa into another rage.

Maria picked at her food, thinking her own thoughts. Only at the last moment, in a desperate cry as the dishes were about to be cleared did she call out, "I shall run away!"

The effect was electric. Motte rushed a hand to her face horrorstricken; John Ashe blushed confusion; Algie grinned stupidly, and little Charlotte drew in her breath and bit her lip. All looked at Papa, who seemed to have turned to stone.

Chapter Three

It was not what Maria had said, it was her act of defiance. The impudence of her eighteen years no parent would have tolerated before the Revolution. In his agitation, Colonel Alston had taken the highway to his ancestral home and reined in his horse at the great avenue of oaks.

No one could tell how old the magnificent oaks were which littered the countryside, their crooked limbs weirdly festooned with Spanish gray moss. Live oaks, the Indians called them, because Indian folklore spoke of their presence long before the coming of the European invaders, long before Charles II claimed the Colony of Carolina in a show of monarchical strength after the setbacks of the English Civil War and Cromwell's brief ascendancy to power.

But William Alston was thinking no further back than his first wedding night when he had triumphantly carried Maria's mother across the portal of The Oaks mansion. Then, he was possessed of such devouring energy for his beautiful bride he so passionately loved. Now, he felt descending upon him an all-enveloping isolation. Then, he had been a dashing captain in wily General "Swamp Fox" Marion's army of patriot rebels, harassing British troops up and down the labyrinth of creeks and forest paths the length of Waccamaw River, gathering recruits from the plantations for Marion's partisan bands. Oh, the exhilaration of those dangerous raiding parties, cutting lines of communication. No British troops ever caught Swamp Fox in all the years of the Revolution, William turned back his thoughts, not even that son of a bitch Colonel Tarleton who his Haggar neighbors had such bitter cause to remember. General Jacques Haggar's patriot partisans surprised by Tarleton's British Legion while defending Charleston, were all brutally massacred. Tarleton rampaged across plantations plundering and raping women. William thought about the treachery of Loyalists joining Tarleton's British troops against their fellow countrymen that sickening day when he had himself come upon a dead woman, ballooning, and flyblown in the sweltering heat, her unborn child cut from her womb. It had been a miracle, two lovers finding each other in that demonic time of hate.

And now Swamp Fox is dead, he thought on; he had died peacefully at his home only last year. Swamp Fox, the patriots' hero, was a beloved senator of South Carolina in the first flush of American independence. And my Mary, too, dead, he thought as he dived his spurs into his horse's sides with unthinking viciousness. His mind was made up. He galloped his suffering stallion back down the gravel road, south through the salt marshes, to Clifton.

* * * * *

Motte found herself between two fires. One part of her envied Maria. Of course hers was a most prestigious marriage she could not deny, but to be a second wife, when only twenty-two years old, to a man eleven years your senior! Yes, she envied Maria and Danny Haggar; she envied young lovers. She studied her face in the mirror. Already her girlish bloom had faded with the strain of continual pregnancies. She could not get used to the unhealthy rice swamps, nor to the breathless humidity.

Hers had been a very different upbringing in Charleston's fashionable quarter before the Revolution. She mused over her earliest recollection, the tragedy of Uncle Miles Brewton, as she continued to gaze at herself. Mama always said it was Aunt Brewton's fault because of her absurd fantasy that their Negro slaves were plotting an insurrection. She had insisted Uncle Miles take the whole family to the safety of Philadelphia. They had all perished when their frigate was caught in a storm off Cape Fear. That's how Mama came to possess her brother's house, the beautiful Miles Brewton residence, secluded from its neighbors by a high-walled garden. That's where she and her sisters spent their happy childhood, until the Revolution, when secrecy and spying was no longer a game. There was one night Motte would never forget.

She was ten at the time, and Charleston had been under constant bombardment for months. Somehow Mama's futile gesture of defiance, throwing flaming arrows through the windows, kept up their spirits. But suddenly the siege was over. Charleston had fallen. That night the house was broken into by British officers. It was one man in particular that had made her blood curl. He drew his sword and came straight for Mama. She and her sisters knew they must not scream and give away the hiding place Mama had packed them into as the enemy hammered at the door. In that moment of terror they watched through a crack. It was the cruelty in his eyes Motte would never forget, and yet his face was girlish. They saw Mama stiffen as the young officer raised his sword. How the look on Mama's face changed his mind, they would never know. Suddenly, he turned and ripped up an Axminster carpet.

Afterward, she learned he was the infamous Colonel Tarleton, who butchered people without mercy. By then, he had commandeered their house and Mama was feeding British officers, but she never let them get near her girls.

Motte was glad her first-born had been a girl. Of course, William was disappointed, but she had since given him two strapping boys. She had named the baby girl Rebecca after her mother. If she had half the courage of her grandmother she would grow into a fine woman. A thought struck her as she reached for her perfume, gently dabbing the sweat from her face, "Will I be content to have my daughter spend her life as a plantation mistress in these unhealthy swamps?" The question remained unanswered, for as she asked it, she heard the pounding of horses hoofs on the gravel outside.

"Why, you are early home," she called, running down the spiral staircase into the great hall.

"I have not been inspecting rice plats today m'dear," said William.

"My poor husband," said Motte. "You look so tired. I will have some tea brewed."

"I'd appreciate that," William said sinking into a chair. "Have Homer come and remove my boots."

Motte saw the look in his hooded blue eyes she found most difficult to combat. She knew instinctively he was going to speak about Maria, and she was not ready for it.

• • • • •

It was a wild idea; but it was the best Maria could think up. She caught Piers as the boys left their lessons. "Walk me to the landing-stage at sundown?" she asked. There was mischief in her eyes which sent Piers's heart pounding.

"Nothing would delight me more," he stuttered with excitement. He had flirted with New England girls, but not with a southern belle and one so full of fire. He felt his pulse race.

"My horse has had a thorn removed. I must inquire after him," she said. "I'll be in the stables. Keep it secret," she said coquettishly before disappearing down the corridor, coming to an abrupt halt as she thought she heard her father's voice. She went stealthily over to the house slave quarters where she found Mauma.

Mauma confirmed the "Maussa" had come home early. You couldn't miss his presence about the house. "De berry idea!" she feigned indignation when Maria mischievously asked her to say, if asked, she was out visiting, but Mauma warmed to the conspiracy.

The sun had not quite disappeared from the horizon when Maria and Piers slipped out of the stables and followed the footpath through tanglewood, safe from observation from the house.

Maria slowed her pace. "*The Prince of Parthia*, you remember I asked if you had a copy?" she said.

"Oh God!" Piers said to himself. "Are we not to speak of love?"

"Well!" Maria continued. "I've heard The American Company in New York is staging it. You Connecticut people—you have the theatre on your doorstep. How I would like to see that play."

"It will surely reach Charleston in time, such a popular romantic-tragedy." Piers said.

"But The American Company in New York is the most wonderful drama group in the world!" Maria said placing her hands together under her chin and tilting her head to gaze at the darkening sky.

Piers swatted a mosquito; his hand-clap awakened Maria from her dreams. They strolled on in casual talk. Piers idly waved a frond to ward off buzzing insects. Abruptly the tanglewood ended and before them an open space, the landing stage, became clearly visible.

"There are no barges!" Piers said surprised.

Maria turned quizzical eyes to meet his. "But there are rowboats!" she said softly.

He flushed darkly under his fair skin. Their hands touched and everything turned to magic.

◆ ◆ ◆ ◆ ◆

William drank his tea in heavy silence. Motte went quietly on with her embroidery, though her brain was afire.

"I will not tolerate Maria's behavior." William spoke at last. "I have loved her from her mother's womb. How could she so insult me?"

Motte raised her eyes, searching his face as if she were discovering her husband for the first time—the hair swept neatly back from the high forehead, eyes proud beneath the hooded lids, the resolute mouth, the sculptured line of the jaw hewn like bedrock. She said, "'Tis but a child you are upbraiding. She has put you in a temper. She will repent."

"But she is not too young to flirt with beaux," said William. "I will have her wed Danny Haggar this fall. It will be a great union between our two patriot families. You will support me in this arrangement." Then he rang for Homer.

Motte felt suddenly faint. William paced up and down the room with a stony face. But it was Homer at the second knock on the door, "Mauma say Missy Maria, she not home. She be visiting."

Chapter Four

As soon as she left the breakfast table, Maria went straight to the library ahead of the boys for their lessons. Piers looked startled as she burst in, their lovers' kiss of the night before still hot on his lips.

"Something dreadful has happened," she cried. "Papa has set a date for me to marry Danny Haggar. Never! Never, never, never will I marry Danny!" She flung herself into his arms. "You must help me, Piers," she cried.

Piers glanced nervously toward the door. Maria's hysteria brought cold terror in his Connecticut veins, where men's fear of witch hunts still haunts. What was she asking of him?

"I have a plan," he heard her say and she seemed to be speaking from a long way away. "Row me to Yahany tonight."

"But it's miles upriver," he protested.

"Oh, don't worry Piers," she said impetuously. "You'll be back by dawn and no one the wiser." For a while she was silent. Then on a thought, she said beguilingly, "If you refuse me..."

Sweat ran down his cheeks from his brow, his emotions in total disarray. He wanted her more than ever. He felt physically tortured. Down the corridor he heard the boys' trudging feet and he was seized with panic. Then one dropped his books with a clatter, and boisterous laughter filled the corridor. "What'll you do when we reach Yahany?" he whispered hoarsely.

"Oh, Piers, you will get me to Yahany!" Maria said embracing him with renewed passion. "Take the Lumberton mail coach to New York. Find Joseph."

Then she rushed for a library book at random and was gone, leaving him speechless, gaping.

◆ ◆ ◆ ◆ ◆

"Yes, I did tell Mauma I was going visiting," Maria had said.

"But you didn't," her father had stormed.

"I changed my mind. I have a right to," she had retorted.

"A right! You have no rights!" Those were his words that really rankled. "No rights! Only duties!"

"Taken a jungle path alone!" he had flared. She knew he believed her. She knew there was not a Negro on the plantation who would ever split. There would have been some unseen black faces — the river boatmen. If any white man asked the whereabouts of another they always said, "I nebber seed nutt'in'."

When they were small, she and Joseph played with the Negro children in the row of slave cabins at The Oaks. Grandpa Joseph forged weapons for patriot rebels, and Mama made cornbread. They were too busy to worry about children and the way they pick up the ends of conversations. "All dis fightin' fuh one white buckra to kill anudder white buckra. Een dey missis, she work wid we on de plantesshun. Yuh r'aly happa sweat ef yuh is wan' tuh eat. We dusn't want de maussa to sell us to anudder white buckra. Dey mus' is cruel peepul." But the Alston plantations were huge domains. Hundreds of Negroes worked from sun to sun, women with head scarves, men with caps pulled low, a whole army of faces she could not name. But oh their singing, vocal choirs winging hauntingly across the rice plats to the rhythm of hand-held hoes lifting clods of clay. Maria had an ear for music. It touched a spring in her. Sometimes she thought their songs a lament which went deep into the soul. At other times they were joyous, especially at harvest when the slave women took the gleanings for their cooking pot and for their scraggy chickens pecking around the rows of cabins.

After she had rushed from the library, as her rage lessened, she became conscious of a Carolina lullaby floating upon the air from the nursery. It was the same one Mauma used to sing to Joseph and her when they were babies. She felt a sudden nostalgia, and with it an unnerving fear of her own bravado. Just as in those long forgotten days, she ran to Mauma for comfort.

Mauma had no need of words. She received her like a child into her ample bosom and felt the tears soak her cotton shift.

◆ ◆ ◆ ◆ ◆

How to tell Maria he couldn't go through with it had agonized Piers the whole morning, so much so that when she slipped up to his room and said the boat idea was crazy, he could not hide his relief. It wasn't the risk of dismissal that had distracted him, as his pupils bent over their books. It was a doubt that gradually formed in his mind that he didn't have the physical stamina for the river trip. These southern boys, he told himself, were tough horse-riding, duck-shooting adventurers, brought up to the treacherous low country. They knew the alligator-infested river banks, the bend of the river and its entangling debris of rotting vegetation; and worse, they were not beyond fighting a duel over the honor of their southern belles.

"You were going to back out," Maria accused.

Piers lowered his eyes. "Not at all," he said. Maria moved over to the window and he ran forward to close the shutters against the sun.

"No, please don't," she said as she raised a restraining hand. Rice plats lay below as far as the eye could see. But, it was not these that caught her attention. She could see her father, stern, erect, astride his horse. The overseer, a short thickset "poor white" from the pinelands, whose wife had fallen victim to the dreaded swamp fever and died before a doctor could be summoned to apply the usual remedies, was speaking to him. "Look how subservient he is," Maria said. "Father owns everyone!"

"But he can't make you marry Danny," Piers stared at the implacable figure rigid on his mount.

"Well, I for one am not for sale!" Maria said adamantly. She thought back over her sobs to Mauma. "I knows what you bin a-doin' gul," Mauma had said. "You t'ink you keep secret from we nigger?" But instead of throwing her into a panic, Maria had been glad Mauma knew without telling. It had taken the burden of deception off her shoulders and she had dried her eyes. She knew Mauma loved her. She knew she would always love her. But Mauma had lifted a warning finger: "Member I hab' de second-sight," she had said.

Slowly Maria turned away from the window. "I've noticed you ride quite often with my brothers."

Piers was disarmed. "Oh, they outride me. They are devils on a horse, afraid of nothing," he said as he ran his hand through his blond waves and shook his head despairingly.

"That's what I propose," said Maria.

"What!" he said as he brought his hand down on the table. "You mean...?"

"Yes, us. We'll go for early morning rides, then one day not return," she said.

Piers paled.

"I'll not return. I'll be on my way to Yahany. When you get back you'll say we raced each other and you lost me," she said as she kissed him lightly. "I must fly. If Papa hears I've been to your room, but he won't," she fluttered, "unless Motte catches me."

Piers' eyes followed her from the room. "Oh, you beautiful butterfly. Please don't get caught," he mimed.

• • • • •

The dawn light reflected stagnant pools on the rice plats releasing a million more fever-bearing mosquitoes from the night's sexual activity. Negro field gangs spawned over the landscape, dark as the dark earth waiting for the seed. An ancient Indian passed like a shadow, the light catching the bluish hue of his hands and legs.

Piers stared after him. "Is he sick?" he said.

"It's dye from indigo," Maria said as she pointed toward the roaring Atlantic. "See those huge vats? They have to wade in the liquid, keep it stirred all the time. Never get rid of the dye. Papa owns them too."

"The net widens," Piers said nervously. "Are you sure you want to go on?"

Maria shivered and hugged closer with one hand her small bundle of clothing.

Piers said, "You're cold."

"It's time for us to part," she said as she pulled up her horse, not admitting to the coldness around her heart, the pitting in her stomach.

"But I'm not leaving you," Piers startled her.

"Oh, Piers don't be ridiculous."

He drew his horse right up close. "I mean it. It's a very rough journey. Overnight stops in shady taverns without your maid? It's unthinkable!"

"But I've left a letter."

"My God!"

"I couldn't do it. I couldn't just disappear without Papa knowing where I'd gone. I told him my plan to lose you and find Joseph."

Piers said nothing.

"He'll never forgive you!" she went on. "He'll throw you out."

He lent across in the saddle, put his hand over hers "I know."

"And Piers, darling, we can't be lovers."

"I know that too."

"What'll we do?" Maria was both agitated and relieved at the same time. She had been afraid of the journey alone and had to summon up every ounce of courage. But she had flirted with Piers outrageously. "Brother and sister? What do you think of that?" he broke into her thoughts.

She burst into convulsive laughter. "You blond Yankee. Why there's nothing southern about you!"

"Same mother, different father?"

"It really is stretching the imagination," they exchanged daredevil looks.

"We'd better hurry. Suppose your father tries to catch us?" he said gravely. "I'm no good with pistols!" he said as he dug his heels into his horse and cantered on.

Maria caught up with him, her face glowing. "Race me to Bull Creek Ferry?" she shot ahead. He chased her. Their daring escapade excited their stallions—manes flew, nostrils steamed, and hoofs crashed through undergrowth, deluging their carefree young riders—all the way to the ferry and the crossing to Yahany for the Lumberton mail coach.

• • • • •

New York was celebrating an early spring; the air was balmy. Maria, exhilarated, filled her lungs, threw back her head with tears of laughter at the sheer thrill of arrival. The journey had been tediously long with so many overnight stops in dirty taverns and post-house inns crowded with bawdy travelers, many lewd advances, and a bumpy coach ride on a muddy road; twice she had had an upset stomach. But, now she knew it was all worthwhile as she drank in the sights and sounds of the beautiful city.

Piers felt exhausted and travel stained. "I long to soak in a warm tub," he said.

"But isn't it just glorious? The heart of theatre land. So much happening. Oh thank you, thank you, Piers. I would never have made it alone."

Piers swung their bundles over his shoulder. His was a sensuous enjoyment, not for New York City which had been a holiday place from his early childhood, but at Maria's happiness which was the successful culmination of their three weeks together. "I'll be sad when we get to Joseph's apartment," he said as he took her arm.

"What'll you do?"

"Stay close by. You never know when you may need your adopted brother," he said good-humoredly. "Stay hopeful," he thought to himself.

"Stay friends," Maria was saying. But she had seen someone.

Piers said, "Who is it?"

"Pa's brother. Hello, Uncle Thomas," she called cheerfully as if it were no surprise.

He faced the two youngsters. He was a neatly dressed burly man who looked more like a wealthy merchant than a planter. "Your father has sent me to fetch you back," he addressed Maria in his southern drawl. "I came by fast packet. I have our return passage booked," he glowered across at Piers.

Piers felt Maria's body stiffen against his arm. Her long silence agonized. He was anticipating her distress with the adventure over and facing her father's wrath, forced into marrying Danny Haggar. She spoke at last.

In her thoughts she relived the arduous land journey. During their travels she had found her own identity and she was no longer "Papa's girl." She released Piers' arm. "I shall not be joining you Uncle Thomas."

"Your father is very angry," he retorted. "If I return without you, well, I don't know what he'll say." He was thinking William should have come himself and left his plantations to his overseers.

"I'm sorry, Uncle. You can tell Papa he has no cause for anxiety."

"You place me awkwardly," Uncle Thomas said bluntly.

Piers said, "The Tonkin Coffee House is around the corner. We can get a flagon of Trent wine to cheer our spirits."

Chapter Five

Young post-Revolutionaries had found an idol. Princeton College debating societies were the breeding ground of their discontent with purblind adolescence their handmaiden and Aaron Burr, New York's irrepressible politician, their seducer. Princeton was his alma mater. Joseph Alston, too, had joined Burr's notorious band of devoted satellites.

Joseph needed an idol. It anchored him. Ever since Grandpa Joseph died he had felt unsure of himself. Grandpa Joseph had come through the Revolution on the side of the Gods, but it wasn't Grandpa Joseph's tales of Cherokee Indian uprisings, horse-stealing, looting, cattle-killing, or shoot-outs. What remained rooted in his childhood's imagination was the stories of the back-country, small-time planters and how they finally suppressed the rule of the jungle only to be oppressed themselves by the big men of the low country. These had been hair-raising stories of wild adventure, escapades of a bygone day before the Revolution. It was Grandpa Joseph and George Pawley's lifelong vendetta that had stayed with him. George Pawley had been England's favorite son; Grandpa had been England's most bitter enemy. They had recruited rival factions in Charleston's House of Assembly at the time of political enfranchisement under the English Crown which was granted only to men owning a plantation of not less than five hundred acres and ten slaves.

Aaron Burr, setting his popularity for the Federalists against the Confederates in new post-Revolution America, inspired in Joseph the same adulation as had Grandpa Joseph.

• • • • •

Uncle Thomas was not used to seedy coffee houses. He had distinguished himself as an officer in General Washington's Continental Army. He had been one of the prestigious few George Washington bid farewell to in the famous Fraunces Tavern off Broad Street after the Revolution. That had been in 1783, shortly before Grandpa Joseph died leaving him "Prospect Hill" on Waccamaw Neck. He had none of William's ambition to dominate the Neck, neither had he been involved in the unrest of impassioned Patriots in rebellious pursuit of Loyalists in their midst while paying off old scores in some of the cruelest aspects of the War of Independence. He had returned briefly to the life of a planter after his father, Grandpa Joseph died, but he had no stomach for it. Instead, he set out to make his fortune shipping the lucrative rice from Charleston and Philadelphia to hungry European ports.

"I want to be an actress!" Maria pushed him off as he brusquely tried to tear her away from Piers. For a long moment he gazed abstracted at his gold-ringed hand from which she had escaped his grasp. It unnerved Maria and she slipped her hand into Piers'. "A thousand horses will not drag me away" she was thinking, when Uncle Thomas looked up with a conciliatory smile.

"We'll go to Fraunces Tavern off Broad Street. You can take a hot tub and change into suitable clothing," he ran his eye disapprovingly over her disheveled appearance.

"But that's the most expensive tavern in New York," Piers ejaculated.

"I have not invited you to accompany us," Uncle Thomas brushed him aside .

Piers flushed. "I have money enough for my own support," he said, stung by the rebuff.

Her fists clenched, her shrill voice cried, "We will not be parted!"

Uncle Thomas scowled his thoughts—the girl is stubborn as a mule! Aloud he said, "I am growing weary of your obstinacy." Although the air was wintry crisp, he mopped with a silk handkerchief beads of sweat that ran down his brow. "But if I cannot persuade you..."

Maria cut in anxiously, "Then you'll sail without me, Uncle Thomas?"

"And meet your father without my charge? I will do no such thing."

Maria's heart sank. She could barely stay on her feet.

"I will remain in New York for a week or so," he continued in his southern drawl, "to keep an eye on you. Besides, I have business." In Uncle Thomas' nature, circumventing trouble was second only to his love of making money, and he was fast turning the situation to his own advantage. "I'll dispatch a courier with a note and await events."

Uncle Thomas' capitulation left the two youngsters openmouthed. Emotionally drained and physically exhausted, Maria burst into tears.

◆ ◆ ◆ ◆ ◆

"Joseph has an apartment somewhere off the Bowery," Maria said. By now, the two men had struck up a kind of friendship, each having been grateful for the other's presence when Maria broke down. It had taken more than a night at the hospitable Fraunces Tavern close by New York Bay for Maria to recover from the fatigue, but her emotions remained turbulent.

Uncle Thomas was getting impatient. "We've been in and out of every dance hall and beer tavern on Bowery," he complained. "Are you sure Joseph is in New York and not at Princeton?"

Maria was not sure. She said nothing. Another hour was spent in fruitless search.

Day dissolved into night and all along fashionable Bowery Boulevard tiny lights beckoned patrons to the beer taverns, when Piers' attention was drawn to a rowdy group of revelers. What he heard as they entered a nearby tavern convinced him they could be friends of Joseph's, a bunch of students organizing a political rally. He followed them inside. "I'm looking for Joseph Alston," he shouted into the shadowy figures in the smoke-laden room.

"Try the parlor," someone said pointing with a coarse laugh.

Joseph philandering? Piers recalled the shy lumbering youth. Southern belles were quite heartless about him. When all at once, there he was mysteriously appearing bearded and brigand-like, a tankard of beer raised to his lips.

"Good God Piers! Got sick of the sight of rice?" he said jovially. "Back to frozen Connecticut already?"

"Maria's outside," Piers replied with brutal truth.

Joseph shot from the tavern, letting fly the tankard, silencing the crowd around the bar to wonder at the commotion.

♦ ♦ ♦ ♦ ♦

Fear gripped Joseph. "Who is dead?" he cried.

"No one. I've only escaped from father!" Maria said with throwaway casualness.

"What! And without a chaperone? You must be mad!"

"Thank God for Uncle Thomas." Maria drew her arm through his and flashed him a disarming smile.

For the time being, Uncle Thomas had let his mission slip from his mind in the heady atmosphere of New York's culture and commerce. Besides, he was flattered by the attention of a beautiful young girl whom he could truthfully show off as his niece.

Then they told their story, Piers and Maria, one talking over the other in the excitement of relating their experiences to Joseph's sympathetic ear.

"My God Maria! You're a rebel after Grandpa Joseph's heart. If he were alive he'd be real proud. Father must be furious. But I can't put you up in my apartment."

"Lend me money?"

"I've a good income from my rice plats at The Oaks. I should be happy to oblige," he said as he entered into the spirit of their escapade.

"Oh Joseph, I knew I could rely on you," she said as she flung her arms round him in a bear hug. "Joseph," she looked up seductively, "get me an introduction, please."

"But I don't have any friends in the theatre world."

"You've got to help me," she pleaded. "I want to learn everything about acting. I want an introduction to the manager of The American Company, to prove to Papa."

"They say there's a deep split in the management, a lot of bad feeling. But I do know they're talking of building a magnificent new theatre, three stories high, with a well-equipped stage, tiers of boxes, a gallery, and a pit."

"Wonderful!" Maria clasped her hands ecstatically. "How can I be part of it? I must! I must!"

Her piercing eyes fixed Joseph's with rapier sharpness. The likeness of her eyes to their father's stunned him. Of course, he said to himself, and out loud to Maria, "I'll talk to Aaron Burr."

Chapter Six

Algernon made an unfortunate remark. "Well Pa," he said, "you can't advertise Maria as a runaway."

"No one has ever deserted from my plantation," William rounded on the boy delivering him a stinging cuff on the ear.

And it was true thought Motte. William managed his plantations like a well-oiled machine. Where was there to run anyway? Not fifty yards from the plantation house, a stroll through lush vegetation was a gift to bloodsucking insects. Even a long skirt was no protection from poisonous plants. Rattlesnakes petrified people, and sneaking in the mudbanks 'gators lay in wait for an arm or leg. Motte remembered one especially horrid day in the stifling heat shortly after they were married. As she languished in the unbearable humidity, a prisoner of her environment, she imagined her sisters happily enjoying the salubrious Charleston sea breezes; she had begged William to let her visit them. But William had been adamant and said she must wait like a good plantation mistress for the annual exodus after the paddy rice planting. Every white planter would then be taking his family to the sea islands for the duration of the sickly season. What a wonderful time it had been, that first reunion with her family and friends.

Thinking back, she told herself she could never have done what Maria had done. It made her resentful. Everyone was talking, and women of a certain age were heard exclaiming, "Without a chaperone too! It's absolutely scandalous!"

· · · · ·

By the next day Joseph began having second thoughts. He had only been one in the crowd of Aaron Burr's admirers. "How can I ask the distinguished United States senator from New York to speak for my sister? He is enormously influential and will probably be scandalized."

"Or be amused. If he refuses to help, you can gracefully retire none the worse for the meeting," Maria caressed his cheek. "For me, Joseph, do it for me. I can't turn back now. You are my only hope."

"How you do pester a poor fellow."

If Joseph had been asking for himself he would have abandoned the idea as being of too little importance to bother the senator. But, spurred on by

Maria, he steeled himself to call on Burr who, never slow to woo a young admirer, showed himself most willing to oblige, even eager to hear more of Maria's escapade. "Clearly an audacious girl of spirit," he had responded with a glint of approval in his magnetic black eyes. And Joseph's crowning reward had been Aaron Burr's invitation to dine at his private Manhattan countryside residence.

When Uncle Thomas heard the astounding news that New York's leading American dramatist and theatre manager, William Dunlap, had set a date to audition Maria, he offered her an entirely new wardrobe, most anxious that she should be suitably attired.

"It won't be how I look, but how I perform," Maria refused to be diverted. Never before had she been so stricken with nerves, not even in the most anguished moments of her hazardous journey north. Finding a copy of *As You Like It* where they were staying, she feverishly began rehearsing before a long mirror—now Celia, now Rosalind.

♦ ♦ ♦ ♦ ♦

Piers waited on the keyside with a small knot of people huddled close against the chilly morning air. Though his eyes were fixed on the packet heaving and rolling, slowly approaching, his mind was not on the reply from Clifton that Uncle Thomas was expecting off the mail boat. "We do not know how your father will answer your failure to return," Uncle Thomas had warned Maria. But Piers had been thrown into a new despair.

Maria had roused every passion in him on their journey together by her brilliant horsemanship, her spirited rejection of the attention of card-crazed men in dirty taverns, her sparkling eyes and infectious laughter at suggestions that she had eloped with her stepbrother and her haughty rebuff at accusations of an incestuous relationship. But Piers had found himself hopelessly ensnared. He sweated out his role with an aching heart to keep to their truce, only to have his spirits dashed at the end of their venture. Joseph had taken Maria over, and Piers could not escape the affinity between brother and sister. Such had been his reward for acting out a false relationship. Perhaps after the audition, he consoled himself, he could tell Maria how much he loved her.

The sloop dropped anchor, and a plank was lowered with a clang breaking Piers' abstracted thoughts. He moved forward mechanically and peered into the faces of a handful of white merchants leaving the vessel, but he knew none of them. Nor did he receive any note for Maria or Uncle Thomas from the ship's captain. He turned back puzzled when suddenly there was a voice behind him.

"I'se bin sen' by de Maussa, Mister Piers, sur. I'se seekin' missy Maria. Oh my, dis place bin mighty big!"

"Mauma!" Piers cried.

"Oh my dis place bin mighty big," Mauma said again her eyes dilated pools of wonder, her expansive bosom heaving, arms akimbo, as she clutched two large bundles.

Piers pushed their way through the jostling noisy crowd. "Migrants are flooding in every day. They say there's near sixty thousand in the city, most with no proper housing, living like rats. But what news do you bring of Clifton?" Piers said anxiously. What mischief, he was thinking, lies behind sending a black slave woman who'd never been off the plantation in her life? If a dowager lady had arrived to entice Maria home he would have been less surprised. What sinister plan had her father for her? He felt unnerved. "Letters Mauma? You bring letters?"

"I git letters. But mister I sho' is w'ary. I'se bin mighty col' in dis place."

Piers turned to face her. "Why, you're shivering Mauma!" He had not stopped to think the crisp wintry air, which Maria and he had breathed in deep like an elixir on their arrival in New York, would be many degrees too cold for Mauma's Negro blood. Waccamaw laid on the same latitude as the Africa from which Mauma's father had been transported.

"An I'se hab no bittle since I leeb de planteeshun mister."

"Oh Mauma, I never thought. That's real shameful of me. Come, give me those bundles. We'll get some warm food and a good log fire over there." He waded across the muddy sodden street to a nearby tavern.

Mauma bent down to remove her shoes now that her hands were free. She did not mind carrying the mud off her feet into the tavern, for her feet she always says, "Blonx de Maussa."

Piers watched Mauma devour a chicken. "Best get you an Indian trapper's fur if you're staying long," he said. "But I expect you'll be going back with the packet," he quizzed her apprehensively.

"I'se git to see Missy Maria first," Mauma said. Her meal finished, she began to take stock of the company around her. "Why mek so all dis peepul mix up?"

Piers laughed at her naiveté. "Because you're in another world here Mauma. See there," he pointed. "That tough guy with the wampum bead belt. He's a Hodenosounee Indian. Mighty tribe these Indians. Should never have fought on the side of the English in the Revolution. But so did half the New Yorkers—Dutch, Irish, German immigrants—many Loyalist traitors resisting the Declaration of Independence."

"What 'bout udder half?"

"Why, they joined George Washington's revolutionary army. But these New Yorkers harbor no grudges. They leave people alone. Plenty of street fighting, mind you, shooting and rioting."

"I nebber seed peepul mix up in all my born days," Mauma fixed an eagle eye on a grinning black face. "I dursent t'ink of it fo we libbin' in slavery. We hab a good Maussa on de planteeshun though."

"You sure have Mauma. But what about the letters?"

"Sh'um in dat bundle," Mauma pointed.

Piers dived forward, untied the bundle with nervous, fumbling fingers. The corners fell apart like a spring released, displaying the bundle's motley contents. There, lying on top, the bold strokes of a familiar pen met his eyes, and he froze with anxiety at the sight of his own name.

* * * * *

"Wounded pride!" Uncle Thomas said. It was as Uncle Thomas had feared. Thinking back to when they were boys William had always taken the initiative, thrived on leadership, been destined for soldiery, proved a brilliant officer during the Revolution with every man in his command a devoted conscript.

But Thomas saw his elder brother differently. He saw how his seething ambition to outshine had distanced him from envious neighbors ever since he claimed his inheritance as a planter after the war was over. No wonder they dubbed him "King of the Neck". And so, William is in everything he touches, Thomas reflected. He has the best plantation, the finest mansion, the neatest rows of Negro street cabins, the jolliest celebrations at annual festivals. He wins the hearts of every soul he possesses to the music of fiddlers, the drummers drumming, and gathers everyone together like a towering white chief over a loyal tribe. How often had he heard William say whenever news of a runaway broke, "No one deserts me. I'm a fair man. I treat my people well."

The shock at his own daughter deserting, his hired tutor a virtual runaway, sprang from the pages of the letter with devastating effect as Uncle Thomas finished reading.

"Poor Papa! I've made him very angry," Maria said.

Joseph turned to Piers. "Yankee, go home! You're a foreigner to our southern ways and I wouldn't rule out a duel!"

"It has crossed my mind," Piers said. But he knew from the other letter which he had kept secret from them that he had no choice.

Chapter Seven

Maria could not stop talking. She went on talking, and he went on staring, never blinking an eyelid. What hypnotized her in her agonized state of nerves was the hat, a black felt hat with a wide brim, which made the famous playwright look more like a bandit than a theatre manager. The setting, too, was macabre, with strange noises, masons building exterior walls, shadowy figures casually hauling timbers across the unfinished stage, someone splashing pink paint onto a vast panel.

"So you think you have talent," William Dunlap cut her short with sudden impatience. He was out of temper. Lewis Hallam had just walked out on him, and his other partner was none too happy. It had been a tooth and nail battle after the War of Independence to bring respectability to the playhouse. He'd had to rewrite his play, the first which he called *The Father*, to point a moral lesson before The American Company would stage it. Mercifully, the comedy had been so favorably received at the John Street that it ran for an unprecedented four performances. He had been ecstatic. He had been lucky, he told reporters in his leading man. "John Henry is a brilliant Irish actor," he had said. Lewis Hallam brought him over when The American Company returned from the West Indies, where it had taken refuge during the war. Well! Lewis Hallam had left the Company, and so had John Henry. If only Henry had not persuaded the English actor, John Hodgkinson, to cross the Atlantic. Hodgkinson, a fine actor, and a tyrannical theatre manager, had completely outclassed him. But would the Park ever have gotten underway without Hodgkinson? The opening date for the new theatre had already been set back by an outbreak of yellow fever in the town.

"I will weary you no longer with idle talking," the cadence was strong, the words tersely echoing through the empty auditorium.

"Ah, Rosalind!" William Dunlap rose to his feet with hands clasped in front of him and eyes sparkling with sudden interest. "A girl of spirit."

Maria's courage took a leap. "I want to be part of this wonderful new theatre."

He liked her down-to-earth manner. "You've been to the John Street of course."

"I went with my brother last evening. We were told the theatre has been rented out to some circus troupe. Gallery hoodlums caused a riot hurling apples and bottles into the orchestra. It was a bit alarming I can say, and there were many empty seats."

"'Fraid the yellow fever scare kept people away."

"Yellow fever?" A spasm of horror ran through Maria. Fear of waking to the discovery of symptoms of cholera or yellow fever, the tragic sight of plague victims dying, was an unending obsession among Waccamaw planters who had a stubborn attachment to atavistic superstitions to prevent the disease. These they earnestly imparted to every child born into low country Carolina.

"Rat-infested wooden shanties swirling in filth belched back onto the land when the bay is at high tide," Dunlap explained. "Our patrons are clammering for The American Company to put on a show at the John Street to take their minds off, transport them to a world of fantasy, but we're waiting for the Park to open. The medics say they've averted an epidemic, but we're all at risk," Dunlap said hoping to deter her.

Maria bounced back, "I am still determined to go on the stage."

"We're closing the John Street at the end of the season. Its wooden walls are dilapidated and audiences are not going to tolerate its poor staging and uncomfortable seating when they can patronize the Park. A sad end to New York's oldest theatre, you may think. I tell you its repertoire includes some of the finest performances you'll ever see, actors and actresses whose names will live forever, but it's had a turbulent history. Learn about it and I'll wager you'll change your mind."

"Never! But I will learn. Someone's got to give me a chance," Maria challenged, when all at once the master craftsman sprang onto the stage and handed her a manuscript.

"Go away and read this. It's my new play for the opening of the Park. There are a couple of walk-on parts."

Maria blushed deep to the roots of her hair falling darkly over her shoulders. Her mouth fell open with no words forming. But he had not waited for a reply. He was already hurrying through the auditorium leaving her staring after him dumbstruck, the manuscript clutched to her heart like a blessing. Only when he had disappeared from sight did she look for a title— *André*! She gave a start.

◆ ◆ ◆ ◆ ◆

Joseph said, "Tell you what Maria. I'll offer to buy Mauma from Pa. Then she can belong to you!"

Mauma had not been eaves dropping. She just happened to be passing by. She was instantly alarmed, walked straight into the parlor and confronted them. "I nebber come tuh stay. I'se fur goin' home."

"Home, Mauma?" For a moment, Maria felt threatened. She intended to keep Mauma with her. She wanted the security of Mauma. How mistaken of Pa, sending Mauma, believing Mauma would succeed in breaking her resolve, but all kinds of anxieties were already creeping into her emotions.

"We'se one gran' fambly," she heard Mauma repeating like an unwanted refrain.

"But it's me you love!" Maria pleaded. Never before had she questioned Mauma's loyalty to her. Never before had she thought of her as a person.

"I knows you bin my chillun eber since you bawn. I calls 'e my chillun ob de Rebolooshun. But I'se fur goin' home." When her master told her to go find Missy Maria and bring her back, she hadn't said anything, but to ask her master to sell her to Master Joseph, that she did not like.

"But your pass has expired," Maria suddenly brightened.

"You'll be picked up by the men who ride patrol if you're caught without a pass," Joseph cautioned.

Mauma stood defiantly before them arms akimbo. "The Maussa send me to fetch yur back. He knows yur giv' me new pass."

"But I am not going back Mauma, not yet anyway."

Mauma began shaking her head slowly from side to side. "Stubborn as the Maussa hissel', dis one," she was thinking. "I'se git to sh'um my udder chillun. Dem lookin' fur me to come home."

"But you haven't any children, Mauma."

"All bin my chillun on de street, Missy. I fur stayin' on de planteeshun. Stayin' in dis place does fret me min'."

◆ ◆ ◆ ◆ ◆

"Gawd knows yuh've sealed yuh fates," Uncle Thomas lapsed into his habit of speaking the Gullah language of the southern plantation Negroes. He peered, old-fashioned-like into each face—Joseph at the opposite end of the table, the diffident adolescent boy behind the grizzly black bearded mask, Maria, her body taut, her passionate eyes defiant, and Piers, he could not abide that pale youth. He disliked Connecticut men, crafty peddlers, self-satisfied Puritans grabbing all the markets in the West Indian islands.

Minutes of silence went by. A servant came to clear the plates. Slowly, deliberately, Uncle Thomas recharged his glass with the delicious White Hermitage from the famous cellars of the Fraunces Tavern.

Suddenly Joseph pushed back his chair. "So, let's drink to us!" He felt good. He raised his glass. "To Aaron Burr my mentor!"

Maria exploded. "For heavens sake!"

"You'd never have entered the John Street without the Burr ticket," Joseph retorted.

"Can't say I like leaving you alone in New York though, Maria," Uncle Thomas intervened. "Your Pa'll be anxious."

"Wish you weren't stopping off in Philadelphia Uncle. Papa will listen to you." Maria paused, her eyes dilating. "Please let Mauma stay with me. She's always taken care of me."

Piers could hardly bear his soul's pain as he listened to her cry of anguish. How is it possible to go on being a girl's friend? The letter he had received from her father had been quite explicit. If he failed to go back, he would be hunted like a common criminal with a price on his head.

"No my dear niece," Uncle Thomas was speaking. "Mauma is not a free person of color. She is to leave by tomorrow's packet."

Chapter Eight

Madam Schroeder's hostelry for aspiring young actresses, on the corner of John Street, prided itself on its good name. Madam Schroeder, a middle-aged widow of ample proportions and solemn countenance, always delivered a little homily when negotiating the filling of a vacancy. It was important to her that her noble connection with New York City should be clear from the start. "If you ask anyone," she was fond of saying, "few will have heard of Peter Stuyvesant." Indeed, it was a constant surprise to her that newcomers to the city did not remark upon its Dutch look, but then, she had to admit that more than a century had passed since New Amsterdam was re-christened New York—and people have short memories.

Although Madam Schroeder could trace her ancestry back to the very first Dutch trading post on Manhattan Island, it was her family connection with New Amsterdam's last governor, Peter Stuyvesant, which she especially cherished. His legendary fiery stand was a characteristic which she liked to observe in her young ladies. But his had been an impossible task Madam Schroeder discovered in the annals. Surrounded by New England colonies with neither money nor men to force back the Duke of York's troops, he reputedly eased his frustration by stumping about on his one good leg and one wooden peg. As each dawn lengthened into day, Madam Schroeder solemnly dedicated herself anew to the Dutch origins of her bustling corner of Manhattan Island.

It was on one of these mornings that Maria Alston stepped across the threshold of Madam Schroeder's residence in search of a room.

◆ ◆ ◆ ◆ ◆

Uncle Thomas frequently remarked upon Joseph's likeness to his Grandpa Joseph. He recalled in his mind's eye that Grandpa Joseph, too, had been an absentee rice planter with no fixed plan for his life. Then, one fine night, he and his friends, calling themselves "sons of liberty," broke into the house of the collector of taxes who had just arrived from London. Masked and carrying firearms, they beat the poor fellow up and left him for dead on the streets of Charleston. The story goes that Grandpa Joseph was never again seen as a powder-haired dilettante in knee breeches, stockings, and shoes with large buckles, idling his time in Charleston's fashionable parlors.

Young Joseph had no rebel cause. Uncle Thomas looked thoughtfully at his nephew lazily drawing upon a fat cigar. Out loud he said, "It's time you stopped roaming around the countryside on that horse of yours. Your trouble is you have too much money."

"But I'm enjoying New York, Uncle," Joseph replied lightly. "And with Maria here, God's 'strewth, I'll be her escort!"

Ignoring Joseph's chivalrous intent Thomas asked, "Has your father never mentioned Grandpa Joseph's friends? Lynch, Middleton, Rutledge, Heyward? All signed the Declaration of Independence in Philadelphia."

"Oh Pa! He talks of nothing but President George Washington's visit to Clifton."

"The year he married your stepmother."

"Exactly so. Pa will go on for hours about the war heroes he invited to breakfast to meet the president, especially the military giants, General Moultrie, and the president's cousin, Colonel William Washington. Was it Rutledge who sent Moultrie a hogshead of Antigua rum in gratitude for his scuppering the British fleet off Sullivan Island?"

"Nobody knows. You couldn't find old Antigua during the war. Must have been smuggled into Charleston harbor. Had already developed a liking for it myself. 'Course I was a boy at the time, but we boys gave false ages and joined the rebel army." Uncle Thomas stared over Joseph's head smiling to himself at unshared memories. "But no more of war talk," he said as he suddenly rose from his chair to make a point. "I think it opportune you should accompany me to Philadelphia. You know it's been the political capital for a good five years now."

"New Yorkers constantly complain of the transfer," Joseph said.

"Come to Philadelphia if you will indulge your political yearnings," Uncle Thomas urged.

But Joseph vacillated and Uncle Thomas got unexpectedly tough. For, unknown to Joseph and Maria, he had received a further letter from his brother at Clifton. "If it is my children's will to exercise their own judgment," William's letter to Thomas dictated, "then let them learn self-reliance without the help of each other's company."

♦ ♦ ♦ ♦ ♦

The feeling Maria had was as if a glass divide had suddenly shattered in front of her, the world she had always known in a million pieces. Marooned, she faced a strange new world. Mauma's going she had finally accepted; Piers she thought brave returning to Clifton to God knows what punishment. Uncle Thomas had never planned a long stay. But Joseph going, that had been the shock. The enthusiasm of innocent youth with all its charged immediacy was lost and in one stroke, adolescence ended.

Today was Sunday.

* * * * *

All that week phantom figures had disappeared behind closed doors, ignoring Maria's presence, always in a hurry tearing off to the theatre or returning exhausted late at night. But, she too felt drained. Only when she picked up the play did her exhaustion vanish. When she began to read *André* by the light of a candle, the plot was so absorbing she could not put it down. So often she had heard her father curse the patriot Benedict Arnold, a high-ranking staff officer who turned traitor during the War of Independence, who changed sides from the American forces to the British and sold secrets to André the British spy. From the opening of the play, André's cry of anguish from his execution cell to General Washington, "Don't hang me; shoot me," the arrival from Britain of André's fiancée pleading in vain for his life and her final madness, the hanging of André. The tragedy so gripped Maria she could not put it out of her mind. She had returned the manuscript to its author full of excitement, but William Dunlap did not respond to her stream of praises. He simply sent her to the John Street Theatre to try her hand at John Hodgkinson's workshop in the dramatic arts. Two things she learned very quickly: this handsome, broad-shouldered, bullheaded darling of the theatre was her adored playwright's actor-manager partner, and he was a brilliant director who was never satisfied.

Maria awoke to the sweet Sunday chime of bells. The air was still with no restless rattle of horse-drawn wagons churning up the boggy earth, fouling the tight-packed clapboard houses on the sidewalks. She could hear Madam Schroeder moving about in the kitchen. Madam Schroeder had already spoken of her conviction, so that there should be no misunderstanding. "The Sabbath," she had said, "must never be polluted by any spectacle of the drama." Though she had added she was not one of those religious fanatics who declared the treading of the stage a crime. "Quite the contrary," Madam Schroeder had said, "I do relish a good melodrama!"

Maria stretched painful limbs, her hands clasped behind her head, and stared at the ceiling. She felt emotionally bruised, physically drained, but she could not dispel from her mind's eye the vision of that towering actor, John

Hodgkinson, who could develop a character in one magical moment to take one's breath away.

· · · · ·

They sent Fanny to fetch her, a thin, tired-looking girl with a wealth of auburn hair falling about her shoulders. Maria stared, fascinated. Holding forth in the center of the room surrounded by attentive young girls sat, like an aged Chinese sage, a woman of extremely advanced years with a haunting walnut-like skin face. With small black eyes, which reminded Maria of currants in a bun, she pinned her like a snake charmer. Maria felt herself wilting under the intensity of her scrutiny.

"Bella is our lifeline!" Fanny said.

A bony finger, from which the flesh had all but gone, beckoned Maria without comment, to squat with the others, leaving Maria disturbed by an uneasy feeling of self-exposure.

Fanny ran through the introductions. "Bella was just giving us a dose of comfort. Oh, the bickering that's been going on all week!"

In a powerful, theatrical voice which belied her wizened frame, Bella said, "The times I have seen an actor held to ransom by a jealous wife."

"We love listening to Bella talk about her stage career. Makes our own struggles seem not half as bad," said Fanny.

"They can bury me under the timbers of the John Street when they pull it down. They'll never lay *my* ghost!"

"Pull it down Bella?" Maria said perplexed.

"As soon as the Park opens. Our patrons have had enough of old sailors' mishaps with scenery changes."

"Sailors?"

"Only a sailor knows how to handle a rope me dearling. Never heard their soft whistle? Way they communicate?" Bella grimaced. "Bloody idiots! There you are on stage playing tragedy with the spectators laughing their heads off as the wrong scene gradually appears behind you. They tell me, girl, you're from Carolina. Would you believe it? I starred in "The Orphan" in Charleston's Dock Street Theatre way back in colonial days. Gawd! Those smoking candles! Whole place a fog! Had an English manager who kept a tavern used by British cavalry men and their mistresses. Gave us a bad name, it did. Would have booted us out if the great fire hadn't come first. Destroyed half the town including our theatre. Burnt down a second time before we got a serious troupe of professional actors."

"What happened to the English manager?" Maria asked hesitantly. "I think the tavern's still there."

"He fled back to England soon as the storm clouds of revolution gathered. Just as that brilliant actor-manager, David Douglass, turned up with his wonderful troupe of English actors. Well, that's another story," Bella said, dismissing it for another time.

"You can't stop there, Bella," Fanny cried. "That's our history!"

"Douglass was a God! He met the anti-British hysteria by calling his players The American Company, but a small group of religious fanatics drove us out of town." Bella slowly let her little black eyes rove around the room. "Gawd! Ma'am Schroeder's a palace compared with those filthy stenching lodging-houses. Small wonder we didn't all die of the plague!"

"You're a real trouper!" her devotees cried.

"Being stage-struck is like a drug that hooks you. You gotta survive. Everywhere he went David Douglass built a theatre which angry mobs pulled down behind us. But Philadelphia, oh, Philadelphia! If I were young again I would follow any troupe to Philadelphia. In Philadelphia we performed *The Prince of Parthia* to an ecstatic audience on the eve of the revolution. Oh, the roars of applause for our first American playwright."

"Thought I couldn't possibly miss seeing *The Prince of Parthia* here in New York," Maria said.

"It's Willy Dunlap's new play that's all the rage. You know the Park's opening with Johnny Hodgkinson starring as André?"

There was a gasp of surprise. "Willy's been handing round the manuscript," Fanny said. "Auditions are not till next week."

"Well, me dearlings! What's all the bickering been about? Only Johnny can play André? But Honora? They'll give the part to Johnny's wife for pity's sake!" Bella turned to Maria. "Me dearlings here are waiting for stardom, watching from the wings the most superb acting you'll ever see. You Carolinians, all us Americans, have fought a long and cruel war for our independence, but in the magical world of theatre the Gods are English still."

Chapter Nine

The day Maria learned John Hodgkinson had run away from home to become an actor was a red-letter day for her. It had been a particularly lively workshop. Johnny Hodgkinson had opened his discourse in praise of Sarah Siddons, rating her the finest tragic actress of the English stage. And then, in a throwaway remark, he said, "How fortunate to have had myself appearing several times in support of her. She writes me regularly of her distress at my crossing the Atlantic." His stupendous self-esteem was like an invigorating tonic to his overworked, aspiring young actors, but for Maria, suddenly finding herself an identity in his own story of escape to tread the boards, there was that little bit of extra.

Then came the break. No more waiting in the wings. Johnny Hodgkinson decided to stage a new production of Willy Dunlap's play, *The Father*. Maria's thrill at getting a part overspilled into tears of joy as she rushed to tell Fanny. "I'm to be Mrs. Racket," she burst in.

"And I, her sister Caroline!" Fanny's face lit up, and they flung themselves into each other's arms.

"Let's go to the Shakespeare Tavern and celebrate!"

"I feel like shouting to the whole world!" Fanny took Maria's hands and they began dancing round the room, when all at once they heard a shrill cry from Madam Schroeder.

"Gawd! She's complaining," they stopped short.

"Maria!" Madam Schroeder shouted even louder. "You have a gentleman caller!"

◆ ◆ ◆ ◆ ◆

It was a rule in Ma'am Schroeder's hostelry that gentlemen callers could only be received in her parlor, if not in her presence. Joseph objected.

"Brother, indeed!" Ma'am Schroeder said as she looked down her nose. "So they all say."

"But truly I am," he had cried after her departing figure.

Alone, he began pacing the room, stopping occasionally to gaze at a wall painting, remarking to himself at the stolid countenance of a Dutch grandee.

The door opened quietly, and he turned, surprised at Maria's hesitant entrance. "Who did you expect?" he laughed, stretching his arms for an affectionate embrace.

"Certainly not you," she said as she ran forward excitedly. "Oh Joseph, how I've missed you."

"I'm only passing through," he said quickly. "You'll never believe it. Uncle Thomas has chained me to Edward Rutledge's law office. He says there's no future in politics if you haven't been admitted to the bar."

"So, you're back in Charleston? You might as well have left the country." Maria fell silent, distracted. She was thinking Joseph must have seen Papa. Her estrangement from her father troubled her. She wanted to excel for him, to prove herself to him. After a while, she asked casually disguising her feelings, "How's Papa?"

"He has a message for you. Since you've decided to assert your independence, he can only hope you'll have recovered your senses and returned home before the Christmas festivities. You know how he feels about family obligations. But I've something else to tell you," Joseph suddenly looked grave.

Maria clutched his arm, butterflies of fear were in her stomach. "Who is dead?" she cried.

"Thank God it didn't come to that," Joseph said. "They've been fighting a duel over you."

"Oh no, Joseph, not Danny?"

"You know our southern boys, Maria. Their seconds say Piers fired wide, more frightened of a lynching from our planter fraternity if he killed Danny than of his own life."

"Piers is hurt!" Maria exclaimed as she rushed her hand to her face aghast.

"It was Danny who challenged Piers to a duel. One morning they went out very early, faced each other ten paces apart, and at the word 'present' a double report was heard and Piers fell to the ground."

"Is he badly hurt?" Maria paled.

"Just a graze above the heart. But all Waccamaw Neck is in a frenzy. It's brought to the surface once more the bitter controversy over dueling. What men will do for love. Remember the number of duels Grandpa Joseph told us he'd fought?"

"How could Danny and Piers be so senseless and risk their lives. Neither has my heart. It's Danny, isn't it? Piers and I are just friends."

"Well then, dear sister," Joseph said as he pulled a package from his waistcoat. The expression on his face told he knew its contents. Maria tore it open with shaking hands. From the scented pages of Piers' formal proposal occurred to Maria to consider their escapade a crossroad in her destiny. Panic-stricken, she handed the letter back to Joseph.

• • • • •

Becoming impatient and a little curious, Fanny went down to the parlor. "We'll not be going to the Shakespeare then?" she said as she made her entrance flashing a smile at Joseph.

Taken aback by the wealth of auburn hair, the pretty oval-shaped face, Joseph said, "You were on your way out? Please be my guests."

"My brother Joseph," Maria said hooking her arm through his, "This is Fanny. We've just been given parts in a play."

"Truly a cause for celebration. I want to hear about it," Joseph said as he turned to Maria. "I'm surprised two lovely girls are venturing to a tavern without a chaperone," he feigned disapproval.

"And here you are," said Maria pressing against him, "come to our rescue."

Fanny thought him an ugly fellow with that awful black beard and those broad shoulders. This was not at all how she had pictured Maria's brother, but she was fascinated by a streak of red in his hair which caught the light from the window.

They found the Shakespeare crowded and were only able to squeeze themselves at one end of a long roughhewn trestle table. It was Maria who let the conversation flow without taking part; her thoughts were far away at Clifton. She saw her father again in her mind's eye as she saw him then from the window of Piers' room, handsomely erect upon his horse instructing an obsequious overseer. She could only imagine their conversation. How many overseers had her father trained at Clifton before letting them loose on his other plantations? But on the Clifton estate, the plantation of his own creation, her father needed no overseer.

She had inherited from him that ruthless single-mindedness which had driven their pioneering forebears not two generations earlier. But she had also inherited some of the conflicting emotions of her mother's high breeding that knew gracefulness, compassion and the value of manners.

Piers had been her God-given way of escape from her father's plantocracy, the female bondage and the wildness in her of an adolescent girl not above a few kisses. She wished she could erase the emotion which plagued her now, the guilt of Piers' passion laid upon her. She knew if she replied Piers would take it as an acceptance.

• • • • •

Joseph stayed on a few days. The city he loved exuded an air of festivity. The yellow fever epidemic had been contained and people were beginning to flock back from Greenwich Village where they had earlier escaped in terror of the disease. Work on the magnificent new Park Theatre was renewed with Dunlap's opening play, *André,* after a series of postponements, now planned for January. The John Street was enjoying full houses by audiences hungry for comic relief after the distressing fever and stench of corpses.

At first Joseph thought it was that Maria had become more mature, and it was not until he had been invited to a rehearsal that he saw her quite differently. It was her rehearsing Mrs. Racket, taking on the character so convincingly of a woman trying to excite her indifferent husband by pretending to have a love affair with a known scoundrel, that stirred in him emotions the like of which he had not previously experienced. His wildly self-centered sister was losing herself totally in portraying someone else's emotional and physical make-up.

"But what tyranny!" he thought. Nothing seemed to satisfy the director. He put the question to Bella, whom he chanced to meet casting a critical eye at the stage from a corner of the auditorium.

"It's been a privilege meeting you," he concluded after an hour long talk with her.

"And I have enjoyed talking to you so much," she had replied. "I love your Dock Street Theatre. After all, I started my career as a professional actress in your hometown. Let me tell you, young man, whatever happens to you in life you will never recapture that first thrill of making your début, your destiny in the hands of the mighty!"

"What an amazing old lady," he said later to the girls.

"She is our Mother Superior!" Fanny said affectionately.

"After a bad rehearsal she's always there to help us get over our emotional upsets," Maria went on. "She just knows what we're feeling because she's felt it herself lots and lots of times. But one thing you'll never get over, she insists, is stage fright."

Joseph raised an eyebrow, "And you still want to tread the boards?"

"Tell that to Papa!"

Chapter Ten

Rehearsals for *The Father* were doomed from the start due to using the John Street Theatre while Thomas Wignell had it rented for the season. Wignell had brought his own company from Philadelphia, playing in Ricketts's Circus. Wignell constantly interfered with Hodgkinson's direction and recalled John Henry's brilliant leading man and his own excellent performance as the comic doctor so much admired by Washington in the original staging of the play. If he had not left The American Company to build his own theatre in Philadelphia's Chestnut Street, he would have sailed to England to recruit his own company.

"But why bring his troupe here?" Maria had asked in despair.

"Sentiment!" someone said. "The John Street will soon be pulled down. He's laying a ghost!"

"If you want high drama!" an old stagehand laughed. "Do you know what all this quarreling is about? Such intense rivalry between the actor-managers? Willy Dunlap's distress at the jealousies among his actors?" He pulled a news sheet from his pocket. "Listen to what the critics are saying. 'Wignell's troupe is superior to our American Company.'"

The odious comparison so infuriated Johnny Hodgkinson that he promptly withdrew his troupe and started rehearsing Willy's new play *André*.

"My *André* will make theatrical history!" he said as he stormed into the Park surrounded by craftsmen making their finishing touches to the building.

The play promptly caught the eye of the storm, still raging these many years after the hanging of the British spy. Instantly besieged by reporters, Willy said he wanted to touch the true spirit of American nationalism with a patriotic melodrama exciting pity, terror, and ultimate vindication of General Washington's execution order.

"Did he write the play for John Hodgkinson?" they probed. "If he had not this brilliant English actor, would Willy have woven his plot around André's contact, the American traitor, Benedict Arnold?"

"And who would play so despicable a character?" Willy answered. "Think of the hissing!"

The controversy surrounding the play reached a feverish pitch. No one could talk of anything else. How would their stalwart, handsome actor-manager, already in his forties, play the slight, sensitive young man, the British spy still remembered by many New Yorkers?

John Hodgkinson went further, citing instances of the adolescent boy he used to see spending his evenings helping backstage at Covent Garden and Drury Lane. "In London," Johnny said, "André lives on as a legendary figure to theatre lovers." And Bella had many more tales to tell of the young British officer's excursions into amateur dramatics in New York halls. How ignominious to be caught red-handed, dressed in civilian clothes, on the road back to the British lines with military secrets from Arnold found in his boot.

Johnny Hodgkinson delved deeper, building up the character of André layer by layer—how the son of a Huguenot émigré trading in London came to leave the drudgery of the countinghouse, took a commission, and sailed for America.

Every leading actress of The American Company auditioned for the part of Honora, André's fiancée.

* * * * *

Her father's letter gave Maria her first real taste of homesickness. "We missed you at the Christmas celebrations. Joseph reported he found you well and I am glad of that..." She drew a picture in her mind. Under a tropical sun, peanuts and chestnuts waiting to be roasted, the Christmas tables "groaning boards" of good fare; and at exactly eight o'clock on the first day of the Christmas fortnight Papa firing a musket to greet the neighbors, and signaling a welcome for all to join in the feasting; the house slaves and field gangs lined up on Christmas Day to receive their "ration of cheer."

The madrigals and singers would peel out the old favorites and there would be dancing. The Waccamaw boys would all be there. Little Charlotte would have decorated the ballroom this year for the first time by intertwining foliage evergreens with fragrant honeysuckle every child knew as "kiss-me-at-the-gate". Why, little Charlotte will soon be having beaux of her own, Maria mused. But Papa had made no mention of Danny or Piers. That was hurtful, but it was how he ended that had touched her deeply. "The memory of your beloved mother restrains my hand against you. I gave the best years of my youth to our patriot rebel cause. You, my first-born, are a rebel without a cause."

If he had left it at that it would have been powerful enough. But there followed a Christmas parcel which clawed her back emotionally, the bond of family she could not break. In the freezing New York winter Madam Schroeder's young actresses huddled together for warmth in their sparsely furnished, unheated rooms. The shared case of fine French reds accompanied by Carolina rice provided a rich meal for everyone. "It's a Thanksgiving, me dearlings," Bella gave the blessing.

• • • • •

The fine building which had been rising during the past year was now on the point of completion. New York was about to challenge the supremacy of Philadelphia. On Saturday afternoon Mr. William Dunlap invited his friends to inspect the interior of the new theatre. One of the most notable features was that there were three tiers of boxes above the floor. The pit seats deserved all commendation. The 'gods' were comfortably housed, and Fontainbleau candle brackets adorned the candlewicks. The theatre was to open January 29 with *As You Like It*.

In high dudgeon, Thomas Wignell had taken his troupe back to Philadelphia and declared he would never again grace the New York stage. The American Company had closed the John Street Theatre. To open at the Park with a comedy, the actor-managers concluded, would ensure a captive audience ready for the company's next play, Dunlap's tragedy.

Harassed actors, rehearsing late, stormed at inept stagehands tangling themselves in a maze of cumbersome wooden pulleys and ropes erected under the stage for props; an entire "ship's crew" fought to change side scenes. A jealous and quarrelsome cast erupted at the least criticism. Johnny Hodgkinson drove himself demented being both director and playing Jaques. In desperation, he pleaded with Lewis Hallam to come back for a fee to be his Touchstone.

In John Hodgkinson's repertoire a rehearsed play withdrawn was no less worthy of his stock of pieces. He had penciled in his notes his favor of Maria Alston's Mrs. Rackett, the arresting force she gave to the part. He decided to cast her as Audrey, the country wench of the forest ensnared by Touchstone's frolics.

"Of course, I'm ecstatic playing against Lewis Hallam," Maria said privately to Fanny. "If only the others weren't so jealous. It's so unfriendly."

"What did you expect, Maria? In the theatre disappointments pile up, opportunity rarely knocks at the door. You may never get another part."

"Oh Fanny, don't be so cruel."

"I would have liked the part," said Fanny.

But Johnny's aggressive direction came as a rude awakening, his continual censure, sudden furies, angry gesticulations. "If I have to break you to make you I will not hesitate!" he finally shouted at Maria before the entire company. "I can replace you at any time!"

It was the challenge Maria needed to find her own ruthless self, the ambition which would not permit failure in her small part as the country wench.

"Play it lightheartedly," Johnny kept up his rigorous direction

It was not Lottie Hodgkinson's leading role as the enchanting Rosalind that excited the foppish young gentleman occupying a prestigious box on the opening night, Lottie's gripping exit line: "If I were a woman..."

The scandals surrounding Sir John Nisbet followed him wherever he traveled.   Town gossips declared him a rascally fellow, while his friends marveled at this devastating Adonis sought after by every débutante in every year. He was rising thirty, still a bachelor, and an unrepentant womanizer.

John Nisbet inherited the hauteur of his French mother with her fine aesthetic features, enticing brown eyes beneath a high intelligent forehead, and mobile crimson lips. He was a dashing figure, always appearing in the latest Parisian style of dress. From his Scottish father he inherited his title. "But my destiny," he was fond of telling his stream of admirers, "is to be rootless."

Every capital city in Europe had experienced his follies, and only when his wild extravagances left a trail of debts did he cross the Atlantic to redeem the family rice plantation. He was equally at home in Charleston and New York, where he had been orphaned as a child.

"I want to meet that girl," he turned to his companions, insensible to the roar of applause for Lottie Hodgkinson's Rosalind. Leaning dangerously from the box, he searched out Maria's face in the flickering candlelight, among the supporting players far backstage behind an exultant Jaques and his brilliant Touchstone.

* * * * *

Now that Johnny Hodgkinson's brother was the licensee of the Shakespeare Tavern, the spacious bar was aggressively claimed the rightful preserve of noisy beer-soaked Park Theatre players. It had never been in doubt that Lottie Hodgkinson would be given the part of Honora, the auditions a farce. "Why, she's a comedy actress!" her jealous rivals protested.   But the "politiking" over the play itself.   New York's battlegrounds had not yet passed into history when half the townsfolk were Loyalists to the British Crown, and half were revolutionary patriots; their skirmishes prolonged the war a full seven years after the Declaration of Independence.

Back in the theatre, chatting in the empty auditorium after a difficult rehearsal, Johnny confessed to Willy his anxiety at discovering it was

Alexander Hamilton, Washington's most favored young officer at the time, who had unsuccessfully entered a strong plea on André's behalf. "He'll recognize himself in your character Captain Bland of the American army. Yes! He can kill the play in one vicious editorial in his *New York Evening Post*. Do you not think the event too close for New York audiences?"

"Our country's honor must be triumphant. That is the message of my play. There can be no concessions for spies!"

"Yet, my interpretation of André will lend sympathy for his fate. I can hear cries of shame when I recite André's famous lines, 'I am reconciled to my death, but detest the mode of it!'"

"But think of the spectacle, Johnny, the tense buildup with the arrival of André's fiancée from England and Honora's final madness—our entire company of players in a triumphal march to witness the hanging."

"For me, Willy, it is a wonderful part. How the play is received will turn on the sensitivities of the New Yorkers." Johnny got up. "I've a dreadful thirst!"

A bright moon lighted their way to the Shakespeare, their heads together still engrossed in discussing the play, when they bumped into a group of revelers. "Why, if it isn't my young friend Nisbet!" Johnny exclaimed. "Long time since we saw you in New York."

"At the John Street if I remember. So, you're pulling the old place down at last. However, I must congratulate you on your splendid new theatre. Some new faces too, eh?" Nisbet said archly. "Your *As You Like It* was terrific!"

"Glad you enjoyed it," Johnny said. "Would you care to join us? We've taken to patronizing the Shakespeare, my brother's tavern."

"Taken it over would be more correct," Willy added jocularly.

"Nothing would give me greater pleasure," came the swift reply.

Chapter Eleven

Of all his dubious traits, John Nisbet's wanderer's ear served him well. "A southern belle, if I am not mistaken."

Maria was just saying to Fanny, "Champion of the Patriots in a crowd scene—Papa would like that." The two girls raised their eyes. In the din of the Shakespeare their shy exchanges were hardly audible when they accepted an invitation to join John Nisbet and his companions for a late supper at the exclusive Fraunces Tavern.

"I must congratulate you on your beautiful performance," John Nisbet finally engaged Maria.

"But the fortune was mine," Maria replied demurely. "The Hodgkinsons are superb, among the greatest."

John leaned confidentially so that she felt his hot breath brush her cheek causing her to catch her own. His eyes were hypnotic. "I was reminded of the incomparable Mrs. Siddons."

Her face aflame, Maria said, "I have heard that in London, Sarah Siddons is acclaimed a tragic actress without equal."

"And so she is," John replied. "But I have also seen her in comedy," he held Maria captive.

Why she agreed to a stroll along the dockside with this handsome stranger, she never knew. The night was bewitching. All across the bay tiny lights flickered from ships at anchor, old women stood in doorways, and fishermen smoked a last pipe lounging on the quayside before turning in.

◆ ◆ ◆ ◆ ◆

Bill postings blared "sensational" and "spectacular". Hostelry windows displayed "no vacancies" weeks ahead.

Johnny Hodgkinson had become so familiar with the character of André he underwent a personality change. As the play opened with André awaiting execution in a prison cell, Johnny infused André with a majestic pathos in a long soliloquy intended to arouse audience sympathy by portraying André, the young artist, with soulful eyes and languishing stature—the dilettante poet, the playwright. He portrayed subtle changes as he was jilted after a long love affair and took a commission in the British army. He showed André's utter incomprehension and dismay on arriving in America at finding a hostile new world, violently anti-British.

Willy Dunlap, watching his play unfold from the auditorium, knew at this point the audience would be fully committed as André, confused and bitter, decided to walk alone from Philadelphia to New York before joining his unit. His reactions to the people he met on the way were brilliantly diverse, bivouacking with odd fellows, sailors, black women, Indian squaws, and deserters.

"Your brooding André is superb Johnny," Willy called. Willy was prepared for the personality change in the second act, when audience sympathy would turn to hate as they discovered in André his low opinion of the Patriots, the Paoli massacre of the American force, André reveling in a shameful victory, looting and drinking with fellow British officers. This, Willy predicted, was going to be a stunning performance.

But when Honora came on stage, looking pale, consumptive, travel stained from a rough sea voyage to appeal for her fiancé's life, Johnny called the rehearsal to a halt quarreling at Lottie's interpretation of the part. "No, no, no!" Johnny disliked his wife's portrayal. The large supporting cast relaxed, lolled against scenery, wandered aimlessly about the stage.

"Lottie's a beautiful actress," the play's Captain Bland said.

"Johnny thinks her Honora is too genteel," someone said. "He wants her becoming hysterical from her first appearance on stage."

"But look at the real life situation," Captain Bland argued. "Her father broke off her engagement to André, by persuading her so easily that André could not afford her. Remember she was a high society girl in delicate health, and André was not of noble birth. Her obituary refers to the fashionable literary salon she gathered around her. She must have had many suitors," the cast poured over the notice Johnny had found while delving into their biographies. "But they kept up a secret love affair by letter," the discussion continued. "Secrecy and a sense of drama would have appealed to André. He must have used all his guile to get Honora to cross the Atlantic to come to his aid. She obviously did love him. Nothing less would have persuaded her to leave England. Worn, exhausted, and frightened is how she would have looked on her arrival. Lottie's wan expression will touch a cord in the audience's heart, arrest the growing tension, suspend imagination. Someone should tell Johnny!"

⋆ ⋆ ⋆ ⋆ ⋆

"There's that dashing fellow again" the cast chatted, leaving the theatre, meeting beaux. Maria flushed as John Nisbet approached her. He had waited at the stage door for rehearsals to end every night for the last ten days then had escorted her to the Schroeder hostelry with Fanny acting as chaperone. But tonight Fanny was off sick.

John Nisbet had fallen devastatingly in love. Maria never imagined her curiosity would lead her into the same delirious condition. She discovered that he owned Dean Hall and recalled its confiscation by the Carolina State Legislature in retaliation for the infernal actions of the British.

"There's no truth in the scandals," he told her lightheartedly. "If after it was restored to me, I had invited Charleston's society girls to frolic and dance at Dean Hall we would surely have met before now. My old grandfather was a dour Scot who left his homeland to transform three thousand acres of jungle into the most desirable rice plantation on Cooper River. He would have turned in his grave."

Maria learned of the fateful journey which left John Nisbet an orphan. His father and mother drowned returning to Dean Hall from holidaying in New York. "They sent me and my brother to Scotland to live with our grandmother, poor dear. She soon gave up trying to discipline me." If Maria had been asked when she too fell devastatingly in love, she would have answered at this revelation—the similarity of their circumstances. Two fiercely independent rebels with no fixed abode like a flash of inspiration falling upon a kindred spirit.

Maria refused to stay overnight in some wayside tavern leaving her bed unoccupied at Madam Schroeder's hostelry, while Fanny slept exhausted from the fever.

"Then I propose marriage. Will you marry me my sweetest love?"

Maria had not expected it. "Clandestinely?" she whispered. He caressed her gently, little by little breaking down her resistance. She felt her strength drain away, her mind trapped in a rapturous time capsule. She sealed her destiny in two breathlessly spoken words.

◆ ◆ ◆ ◆ ◆

Crinolines, exotic silks, and the latest Paris fashions adorning the cream of New York society, set the tone of the opening night. The atmosphere was heady with expectation. March temperatures were leaving crisp wintry days behind; summer's intolerable heat and humidity were not yet ushered in.

Prominent in the packed house at the new Park Theatre sat Alexander Hamilton of the *New York Evening Post*. Hamilton's concern over the hanging of André was well-known. Hamilton had been George Washington's favorite twenty-year-old legal aide at the time the general received warning that one of his American generals had defected to the British. Hamilton, the gullible youth given to fine rhetoric and the charms of beautiful women, refused to believe Benedict Arnold's wife, Peggy, capable of complicity in the treason. His mercy plea that General Washington spare the British spy from hanging was unsuccessful.

William Dunlap watched Hamilton's sharp eyes search from the shadows of the candlelit auditorium for familiar faces as seats were occupied. Hamilton was always aware of his public image, his distinguished career as a lawyer, writer, and first secretary of the treasury. Dunlap wondered whether Hamilton, nearly twenty years on now, would recognize his thinly-disguised character in the play's brash young Captain Bland.

The curtain opened, with André alone on stage against a backdrop of a prison cell. Could this diminished, tragic figure be Hodgkinson, their robust Shakespearean actor? He was motionless for a full electrifying minute. Slowly the figure uncurled from a stool, center stage, and began a long soliloquy preparing for the kind of death he must face. And John Hodgkinson knew he had his audience captive, women were moved to tears.

The scene was changed with spectacular dexterity, and the audience was presented with George Washington in lively conflict with the romantic young Bland.

"He saved my life once," Bland pleads for André.

"America's honor must be satisfied," Washington insists on hanging. Bland hurls insults at the general, and tears the cockade from his helmet.

Never for a moment did Willy dream allowing his character to behave so atrociously would cause a riot. The audience leapt to their feet, hurled abuses at Bland, pelted him with rotten fruit, demanded his blood. Stagehands nervously rushed on another scene as Willy looked anxiously across at Hamilton who was busy scribbling something on a notepad. The stage cleared, the glory of America triumphantly upheld, the audience resumed their seats, and the play continued.

Honora came on stage to plead for her lover, and the pace changed. She won the hearts of the audience with her sensitive appeal. They loved her because she was a beautiful actress. The pace quickened. The unhinging of her mind was a terrorizing piece of acting. She was make-believe *par excellence* for her adoring audience. She could never have existed in real life but she had created life in a brilliant performance. The audience rose again, this time in tumultuous applause not of Honora, but of Lottie Hodgkinson.

Willy Dunlap was again put about. Had the audience lost their way? Had Lottie stolen the show? A brief interval was called. And when the second act began, no one was left in any doubt of the moral issue and patriotic content of the play as Johnny's André at the gallows, excelled Lottie's Honora, in a crowd scene of nerve-shattering vitality and spectacle as had never before graced the New York stage.

Chapter Twelve

Maria insisted on secrecy, and after a fashion, they succeeded. But Madam Schroeder had to be told. In the flat of an absent friend, John and Maria's furious lovemaking blinded them to the scandals spreading like wooden buildings blazing in a New York suburb—until Johnny Hodgkinson threatened to replace Maria in the gallows scene. It was not what Johnny wanted. Maria's partisanship in the crowd scene as the second act moved to a rousing climax had all the melodrama of a true patriot. The audience would expect nothing less.

John Nisbet was aware that he did not love Maria. Their clandestine marriage had appealed to his rogue genes. He had subdued a southern belle, renowned for her haughtiness, and this touched his vanity. He admired her strength, her defiance of convention, and the way she passionately made love, giving herself without fear, without regret, commending herself body and soul, which summoned all his reserves of sexual appetite. He thought of himself returning to Paris as a married man reveling in the notoriety—the most desirable bachelor in the whole of Europe suddenly appearing with a nineteen-year-old bride who had brazenly trodden the stage, and had placed herself among the outcasts of society. But, there was something else. Maria had spoken endearingly of her wealthy brother.

The *New York Evening Post* gave *André* a cool reception and declared the event too close. The play was not a popular success and it ran for only five performances. John Nisbet thought it providential. He wished to escape the awful summer pestilence and New York's intolerable heat. "We will honeymoon in Europe, my little beauty," he said, "where you will find the very latest in fashions."

But Maria had just seen something else reported in the *New York Evening Post* which riveted her. " 'Many will remember,' " she read, " 'the South Carolina Jockey Club match race between Sir John Nisbet of Dean Hall, and John Randolph of Roanoke. John Randolph won the race, but John Nisbet captured the hearts of many enamored fair ones, a very elegant gentleman.

> Shaped for sportive tricks,
> And made to court an amorous looking-glass,
> Capering nimbly in a Lady's chamber,
> To the lascivious pleasing of a Lute.

It is rumored Maria Alston has won the prize, Colonel Alston's rebel daughter.' " Maria pointed to the notice with a shaking hand. The written word brutally ended the fantasy world she had been indulging. She knew instinctively the day of reckoning was about to overtake her.

"Well it had to come sooner or later," John said casually, enjoying the allusion to himself with a rascally expression on his face.

But Maria was serious. "Papa never misses the races. He will remember your match."

"I do recall Colonel Alston's presence, a formidable competitor. He took the Jockey Club purse in the two mile heat, beat General Washington's Telegraph with his horse Alborac, in a good race."

"We must make peace with Papa. Go to South Carolina. Go home, John, to Dean Hall," Maria gestured dramatically.

"How now my beauty? Would you deprive us of our honeymoon?" John stroked her hair and entwined it in his fingers.

"My mind will not be at rest." Maria pleaded. "Then we'll travel to Europe my love, stay as long as you like. I think you've made me grow up."

"I don't think I want you to grow up my beauty," John began to lose patience. "Anyway, your brother is expected in New York this evening."

"Why didn't you tell me?" Maria's eyes flashed. "Joseph coming? That's wonderful. We can travel home together. Joseph will support me."

John said nothing his thoughts behind the elegant features inscrutable. He had kept his invitation to Joseph secret. He needed to win his brother-in-law's goodwill, here, in New York, playing upon Maria and Joseph's familial affections. He looked for a substantial purse of money as a wedding gift. Then there was the trip to Europe.

* * * * *

" 'A gentleman from Britain with no riband to mark him a patriot?' " Joseph mimicked his father. "Pa is absolutely furious! He is threatening to alter his will."

"Oh no!" Maria said, agitated. "How can we placate him? Surely he won't disapprove when he sees how deliriously happy we are."

John Nisbet did not like the threat either. "I will make amends by formally asking for his daughter's hand, if it will please him."

Joseph laughed. "Don't mock him. That he'll never forgive!"

Maria looked from one to the other. No two men were less alike in stature, grace, and intellect. John is popular with the turfites she told herself. "Everyone knows Pa has the best stud on Waccamaw. Talk to him about horses, John, especially his famous stallion, Gallatin" she said. She turned to

Joseph. "When John and I are settled at Dean Hall I shall take my proper place as plantation mistress."

"My dearest sister," Joseph said astonished. "How you have changed!"

"No sir," John interjected. "I intend to take my little beauty to Europe, where we'll honeymoon in Italy."

"And a fine pair you'll make," Joseph said awkwardly, envious of Nisbet's easy charm.

"You don't understand, Joseph. I need Papa's forgiveness."

Joseph thought for a moment. "You should go to Clifton. What other choice have you?"

"You are my wife!" John Nisbet rounded. "I refuse to change our plans." But their unyielding expressions caused him to rethink. He had yet to receive a purse. "Oh, very well. I'll consider it," he gave a casual wave of his hand. Before either could respond he added, "Why don't we throw a party to celebrate Joseph's arrival? Invite Willy Dunlap, the Hodgkinsons, Fanny, Bella, absolutely everybody!" He took Maria's face between his hands and said, "To mark your retirement from the theatre my little beauty."

"Brilliant!" Joseph said. "I'll make you a belated wedding breakfast present."

"Oh, Joseph, it'll be magnificent!" Maria hugged. "You'll be one of Bella's favorite dearlings."

John said, "We accept with pleasure."

"But, I'll never never lose touch with the stage," Maria disengaged herself with a histrionic gesture of defiance.

Just then a thought occurred to Joseph. "An invitation to Aaron Burr might not go amiss," he said.

♦ ♦ ♦ ♦ ♦

The sense of unreality about so much that had happened to her was heightened by the remoteness of the southern plantocracy. As she retraced her steps, passing from one post-house inn to another overnight stop, taking the long land journey back to Yahany, it was impossible for Maria to strip the treading of the stage of its romance, because it had been a profoundly moving experience.

Tavern keepers, who remembered the high-spirited girl innocent of the emotional problems she was causing her fair young escort who angrily rejected lewd inferences of whoredom, today fawned over the newly wed Lady Nisbet as if they had never before set eyes on her. Sir John Nisbet, gentleman, gave an air of respectability to their dubious premises. Besides, they were receiving generous rewards from Mr. Alston junior for clean private rooms, servant girls, and good meat and drink.

However, Maria felt an acute sense of loneliness. She had taken part in an historic event, the staging of *André,* and she had not realized the significance until after they had left New York. She would carry away images, idols she would worship for the rest of her life. Amid all the bickerings, the rivalries, the chaotic conditions in the theatre, terror in the wings waiting to go on stage, audience abuse, she had been in the presence of genius—the Hodgkinsons and Willy Dunlap. And she had been touched by a little magic.

Chapter Thirteen

Round a bend, in the haze of dust from the rough dirt road they had bumped along for an interminable number of days, the Alston chaise awaited them. Maria gave a cry of relief.

"So this is Yahany!" John Nisbet complained bitterly, stepping from the mail coach with stiff limbs, fastidiously brushing dust from his clothing.

In the Alston livery, the coachman sat proudly erect on the box. Joseph looked puzzled. "You're Thomas, the horse boy."

"Ole coachman git de brownkitties. 'E git so wet his skin sprouted watercresses, please Suh, Maussa." A broad grin showed Thomas's white teeth gleaming in a coal black face, fresh with youth. He tightened his grip on the reins of the four beautiful long-tailed bays. Hearing again the Gullah dialect she had learned as a child from her plantation nurses, struck at Maria's heartstrings. Memories started crowding in.

As Thomas cautiously turned the chaise homeward, the first intimate glimpse of the rice river came into view through the forest foliage. Then a flight of herons rose, and Maria watched their ascent in silent ecstasy. She had not known how much she had missed her beloved southern low-country. Still, the anticipation of arrival filled her with dread.

Joseph pointed out The Oaks as they passed. "My main source of income," he said.

Nisbet nodded without comment. Maria slipped her hand in his and felt him taut beside her.

* * * * *

William Alston of Clifton savored a glass of the Madeira wine he imported by the pipe. Two stalwart Negroes stirred the oppressive air with large peacock fans. Outside, humming cicadas greeted the night, while fever-bearing mosquitoes bashed in vain at the tightly closed shutters.

"Some of my own friends were brutally slaughtered by treacherous Loyalists," he said bitterly. "Maria has deeply wounded me with this clandestine marriage to a Briton."

"We must not be unwelcoming," Motte urged, "or she'll turn away from the family." She knew how deeply her husband had been longing for Maria to come home, and that he would never show his feelings under that thick façade. She rose from her embroidery to place a loving hand upon his shoulder. "Try and forgive her. Think of it," she appealed to his regard for his public image. "It will be the biggest news-story in Charleston!"

♦ ♦ ♦ ♦ ♦

As they came into sight of Clifton, John Nisbet exclaimed, "Why the plantation house stands on a sand hill. It's imposing high!"

Maria tensed.

"You are trembling my little beauty," he said as he took her hand. He was glad the journey was almost over. He hated this landscape with its tangle of rice rivers, the dense vegetation, and everywhere hanging fronds of ghostly gray moss.

Suddenly, Joseph pointed. "There's Pa galloping like a madman towards the King's highway. God's teeth, Thomas, rein in the horses!"

Joseph descended from the chaise and helped Maria out. John Nisbet did not move.

This was how William Alston wanted to meet his children—contrite at his feet. Maria dragged her eyes up to his and grabbed his stirrup for support. She felt faint, unnerved by his silent scrutiny and the steely blue eyes beneath the hooded lids she had dared to defy in the wildness of her teen-age. Would he never speak?

Colonel Alston had not known till he looked again into the face of his first-born that he had spawned his very likeness. Only death can separate us, however far she tries to run, his subconscious told him. He dismounted and opened his arms to receive her. Drained of all conflicting emotions, she let herself be clasped like a child. "You have come home, my beloved little daughter," he covered her with kisses. "Oh, what lamenting you have caused me!"

"Oh, Papa! I love you! I love you so much!" But suddenly she drew back. "I cannot stay. I am wedded and I love my husband. Wherever he goes, I will go. Please Papa! We are desperate for your blessing!" Maria turned toward the chaise and smiled anxiously at John.

But her father had remounted. With lightening dexterity, he swept her into the saddle across his knees, cradled her against his chest, and galloped back to the mansion without a word to the two astonished men left standing.

♦ ♦ ♦ ♦ ♦

Cheering family crowded the piazza in front of the mansion, joined by hand-clapping house servants. Slipping embarrassed from her father's saddle, Maria went straight to give Mauma a big hug.

"I'se bin 'specting yuh," Mauma grinned from ear to ear.

Motte stepped forward. "Dearest Maria! I'm mighty glad to see you."

"Why, Motte," Maria said as she looked down at four infants tugging at her skirts gazing wide-eyed, "another little stepbrother?" They kissed on either cheek. Maria thought her stepmother had aged.

"Three sons she has given me," her father interjected proudly.

But Maria was embracing the grinning giants, John Ashe and William Algernon, and laughing affectionately at Charlotte, a gangling schoolgirl, squeezing excitedly between the boys.

"What a charade!" said a voice from behind in an unfamiliar accent.

Colonel Alston turned enraged and said, "The impudence!"

John Nisbet bowed low. "I beg your indulgence, sir. It is my wife you carried off!"

"I do not recall your asking for my daughter's hand," the Colonel said as he straightened, his dark hair, swept back in military fashion, antagonism in his heavy-lidded eyes, a sneer in the upturned corners of his resolute mouth. "I am aware you are a gentleman lately from the Kingdom of Great Britain, and not to be taken seriously excepting on the turf."

A stunned silence greeted his remarks, every pair of eyes strained fearfully in his direction.

"Then I ask for her hand now, sir, formally," John Nisbet bowed ingratiatingly. Needing to finance this expensive sport, he had tenanted the property he had inherited in Scotland's illustrious suburb of Edinburgh, the House of Dean. However, this did not begin to cover his costs or the burden upon him of the lands and Negroes of his Cooper River rice plantation. He needed desperately the favor of Maria's immensely rich family.

"You have placed me in an invidious position. I declare you a knave!"

Maria rushed forward. "I, too, am guilty of the deception, Papa! Will you not hear us?" she pleaded.

◆ ◆ ◆ ◆ ◆

After a refreshing tub, Maria's spirits rose. She put on a pastel-colored muslin. John, in immaculate dress after his own tub, covered her soft white neck with amorous kisses. He ran his eye appreciatively down the elegant gown falling in gentle folds to her slippered feet.

"Lady Nisbet!" he laughed. "As soon as my pretty little wife presents her husband with the dowry, we can take to the road." But there was no laughter in his eyes.

Maria said nothing. She put her arm through his, and slowly they descended the broad stairway.

Impatient to give the word to raise glasses, they found her father pacing the piazza, the family nervously standing by. "Good gracious, Maria! I see you have grown into an attractive young lady," said her father.

"And with a title, too Papa. Does that not please you?"

Homer stepped forward with the punchbowl. With the glass of the lime punch, the muscles of her father's face relaxed. Maria moved away to sit with Motte, and they fell to gossiping.

"So distinguished looking!" Motte said approvingly. "I look forward to visiting Dean Hall Plantation as soon as you are settled in your new home." But Maria was not listening for her husband had just said, "I do not engage myself as a planter." She winced at the reaction, Papa rose to his full height, and melodramatically waved his arms at his vast estate, rice lands as far as the eye could see. "I culled three hundred prime slaves from the estates of planters facing financial ruin through neglecting their plantations!"

"It is true Dean Hall Plantation yields only a meager profit. You may know, sir, my brother Alexander, arriving from Scotland found the marshes, creeks and swamps so unpleasant, his energies so sapped, his temper so frayed that he demanded his half-share of the Negroes and stocks on the plantation and went in search of a healthier spot."

"Am I to understand you also are burdened by debt?"

"I was forced to sell a prized plat of land in Charleston left me by my grandfather."

"But the estate remains intact?"

"Indeed, sir," John looked hard at Maria. "I am anxious to get home. The Dean Hall estate will have a plantation mistress, and none finer than your own daughter."

Maria watched, with lowered gaze, her father drum his fingers on the arm of his chair. The air was tense with waiting. "Hmm!" he spoke at last. "I had planned a union for my daughter with one of our leading patriot families."

Chapter Fourteen

Sitting on her father's right-hand at the huge oak dining table, Maria was as nervous as if she were about to go on stage. She desperately wanted him to understand the new American drama was appealing to the spirit of nationalism, that it was respectable to be in the theatre nowadays. "Papa," she said, "I have been privileged to see great acting. I wish you could have seen the famous English actor John Hodgkinson play the part of André. You should have heard the applause!"

"André the British spy? I applauded Washington's decision to hang him. Some damned loyalists wanted revenge. Traitors all!" Maria's enthusiasm touched a mainspring. Treachery which nearly lost the patriots the War of Independence never failed to rouse him.

John Nisbet wanted to hear more of their conversation, but young William Algernon seated across from him attracted his attention asking about the culture of rice at Dean Hall.

"I leave everything to my overseer," Nisbet replied.

"And you say the plantation gives meager returns? Why man, you should check the trunk-minders. The overseer is probably drowning in lime punches with no master at his heels," said Algernon.

The boy held him with very intense eyes. Nisbet was impressed by his features, much finer than Joseph's, the thin line of his eyebrows, long nose, mischievous mouth, clean-shaven pointed chin. His precociousness irritated him. "Why, the lad's nearly half my years," he was thinking. "You take a mighty interest in my affairs," he said out loud.

"Does your overseer see the rice fields are carefully bunded and graded?" Algie went on relentlessly. "The trunks..."

"Trunks?" Nisbet interrupted.

"Why the floodgates man! Everyone knows they're called trunks! Two facing doors set at intervals in the big earth banks. The trunk-minders lift the outside door to flood the rice fields on the freshwater tidal flow. That'll push the inside door open."

"Too complicated for me, boy. My overseer's a poor white from the pinelands, but he's bright. Got a pretty wife too," he added, picturing the willow-like girl he'd flirted with a few times.

"Well," Algie persisted, "if the trunk-minders let any salt water on to the rice fields it'll kill the rice. It's a mighty skillful job being a trunk-minder. And if they let too much water on the fields the rice'll drown. If the fields are not properly graded when they take the water off they'll leave stagnant pools. No rice'll grow where stagnant water lies. They're simply a marvelous breeding ground for mosquitoes. Meager returns you say? Have the earth banks checked. They may not be properly sealed against alligators, rats, and snakes."

"I will, I will," Nisbet said dismissively, letting his eyes rove around the table. He was a stranger to this family reunion. He had no sense of family himself. He never bothered to keep in touch with his Scottish cousins, or to visit his brother Alexander. "What undertones of mistrust lie behind their conviviality?" he was thinking. He tried to catch Maria's eye. Once the dowry is paid...

· · · · ·

The family, up at the big house, was getting ready for the annual migration to Charleston and their sea-island summer house. Even among the field hands there was an air of expectancy. Ned, the Negro driver, had been at Clifton plantation from the start, bought by William Alston from his father's estate, The Oaks, where he was born in Grandpa Joseph's time. Ned was proud of saying, "When de Maussa move to Clifton, after de war, an' git all dem prime slaves mix up from udder places, I'se teachin' em 'bout de way he do t'ings an' dey soon settle down."

It was May the first and all along the Waccamaw, white planters and their families were moving to escape the dreaded rice fevers as temperatures and humidity rose unbearably. Once again, the slave community, left to face these dangers from which they were no more immune, would count their dead. On the Clifton plantation, Ned braced himself for the sickly season which coincided with the heaviest period of work on the rice plats. Sometimes he had to threaten a lazy good-for-nothing with short rations; but never with a beating. "Dat not de Maussa's way," he would say when a field hand complained about some laggard. "Dat why de Maussa happy to leave de planteeshun wid me when he flit to de races. All dem ebony backs bent double grubbing out de weeds choking de sprouted rice plants, but no task too hard. I'se hear bad t'ings 'bout de driver at The Oaks now' days, beatin' slaves fur not finishin' de task. But dat place git no Maussa libbin' on de plantesshun, an' de oberseer he be dat cruel." But it was not the onset of the hot season, the usual packing up for the holiday, that was causing all the excitement.

· · · · ·

"Nisbet has told no one of his marriage," said William Alston. "They heard about it by accident. Now they are inquiring about the girl and the family. Their insinuations are a gross insult!"

"And who are they to question?" Motte fueled his wrath.

"Cousins and a guardian in Scotland residing at the House of Dean, the ancient family seat outside Edinburgh. He also admits to a great uncle in New York that he has not visited in years. I have advised Nisbet to send his uncle a peace offering. I have offered a pipe of wine matured in oak. He has expressed his gratitude."

"You have to like him," Motte said wistfully. A gentleman of her own age she could imagine as a suitor, seduced by his charm. "Maria, too, has been very hurtful," she reminded her husband.

"I know my daughter and I forgive her, but I will not tolerate Nisbet's relations questioning the gentility of Maria's connections. I will have them know I am the richest planter on Waccamaw, and that I own the finest property in Charleston. I will have them know I am a member of the South Carolina State Legislature, party to the confiscation of their plantation during the war for its British connection. From what I hear, their plantation has never prospered since Mr. Deas of Carolina got it back for the family with all the slaves after the war."

"What do you intend?" Motte asked guardedly.

"I have told Nisbet I want to know if Mr. Deas is a good and honest manager. Maria will bring to him a very substantial dowry, and if the estate continues to give meager profits, I will send some of my own Negroes. Maria will soon discover the worth of Mr. Deas."

Motte showed sudden concern. "Will the newlyweds go straight to Dean Hall rice plantation and stay up there on Cooper River during the sickly season? Will they not join us in Charleston, breathe the salubrious sea air? Attend the annual St. Cecilia Ball?"

"Nisbet says he wishes to make a short trip to Scotland. He assures me he can command a safe passage. I pray for Maria's safety."

"Oh but how exciting! A trip to Europe! Maria will wish to travel to London to see the great actress Sarah Siddons play one of her famous roles at the Drury Lane Theatre. However will she settle to a life of domesticity when she returns?"

But William Alston had other thoughts. He forgave, but he could not forget. "To let herself be spliced to a gentleman with no riband to mark him a patriot!" he said for the umpteenth time in her hearing. "I pray no evil will come of it."

Chapter Fifteen

It was because she had been away from the South that Maria developed an attitude. When she was growing up, she woke to the familiar thud of pestles and mortars, women pounding paddy to remove the outer husk and the swish of the fanners' baskets separating trash from the clean rice. From her window she could see in the street the mass exodus of slave cabins to the fields. All her father's Negroes, necessary for the intensive hand-culture of the paddy rice, snaked single file to toil in his acres of steamy swamps. Echoing through the house, she could hear Negro spirituals soothing fractious children, the Gullah chatter of house slaves and their peals of laughter, Homer's voice scolding, and Motte's modulated tones giving orders with aristocratic dignity. A new day, a new surge of energy unleashed before the blistering sun rose too high. When she was growing up, Maria had no more attitude to the plantation south than the seabirds have an attitude to the rolling Atlantic Ocean over which they fly.

In New York, in the turmoil of a busy port, all kinds of people were doing their own thing; the city was lonesome. She had come back a woman. She could not explain it to herself. She had developed an attitude which embraced respect for family; that was her attitude when John Nisbet carried her impudently across the threshold of her new home.

• • • • •

"Oh what a truly imaginative setting," Maria exclaimed. "Why it's like a village, and not like a single plantation at all. Everywhere is so neat and clean."

"Ah, my beauty, my agent, Mr. Deas, serves me well. I leave the culture of rice to the overseer, but I use my Dean Hall plantation house as a hunting lodge. My houseguests find the view breathtaking, and the amenities to their liking."

Maria gazed beyond the village of slave quarters and was enchanted. The Cooper River moved sluggishly. From its other bank to the horizon, newly sprouting paddy rice waved emerald in the breeze. "If I am to be mistress, I should like to be acquainted with Mr. Deas as soon as possible."

"After our trip to Europe, my beauty. Tomorrow, we will continue our journey to Charleston. From there, we will embark for North Britain."

It was the change in his voice, an unaccustomed hardness, which sent panic coursing through her veins. "Why the haste?" she protested. She had found romance, and she did not want to travel further. Besides, she had something she must tell him.

John Nisbet thought back to the ensigncy his guardians had purchased for him in the 59th Regiment stationed in Gibraltar. Major Cochran had called him an indolent Adonis, for in pursuing the game of love he had soon exhausted his pay and allowance and had so burdened himself with debt he sold his ensigncy. Many times since had the burden of debt shackled his liberty. He was not prepared to resign this freedom, bought with a substantial dowry, to obey at Maria's feet.

* * * * *

Owls hooted, alligators barked, and the silent marshes stirred from sleep in the moonlit night. Maria broke her news. Lying together like two forest animals, she whispered, "We're going to have a child! I think I am the happiest woman on earth!"

"Then our child will be born in Britain," he stunned her.

She swung from his arms, and laid her hands flat upon the great four-poster. In the moon's light she looked pale, her dark hair falling in long ringlets screening her breasts. "The times are not propitious," she said impulsively. "The West Indian sugar islands are seething with insurrections."

Seductively, he drew her back into his arms and spoke to her of Paris, of love in Paris, and smothered her with kisses. "We can go north by the Orkneys to Leith with complete safety," he said softly.

"I shall not step from these shores till our child is born. He will have no British birthright."

"He? So we are to have a son? And why should he not be born in North Britain? Heir to the baronetcy? *That* is his birthright!"

"Please, please, my darling, wait another season," Maria said as she seized the hairs on his chest with clenched fists and dissolved late tears.

"If you will not accompany me as my spouse, I will travel alone." He reached for the sheet kicked aside in their feverish lovemaking, and took a corner to wipe away her tears. "My little beauty, spoiling her face?" he said as he kissed her cheeks, her nose, her mouth, her neck. She yielded to his fondling.

* * * * *

Hearing of the stupendous dowry Maria had brought her husband, social gossip confirmed suspicion that the turfite dandy had married primarily to lay his hands on Alston wealth. But for a young husband to desert his wife while she was carrying his child, that was an offense against all the proprieties.

Waccamaw planters arriving in Charleston to escape the dreadful summer heat and bilious swamp fevers were excitedly opening up their town houses for the high season of music and dance; the Alston family was already in residence in the fine, all-brick Miles Brewton house boasting long windows and double piazzas to catch the salubrious sea breezes. Soon, friends and guests in their exquisite brocades and powdered wigs, would attend the ever-popular Alston musical evenings in the beautiful drawing room with its magnificent chandelier suspended from an elaborate cove ceiling. "This was the dowry I brought to my husband," Motte was thinking, "this beautiful, beautiful property." She could smell the azaleas as she sat at her writing desk and breathed deeply, joyously.

Joseph came into the room. On seeing him, she picked up a note from her writing desk and handed it to him exclaiming, "Oh, it's so embarrassing!"

He said nothing. He had never been one of Nisbet's hunting fraternity, never visited the Dean Hall Plantation on that bend of the Cooper River dividing east and west. He had offered to take the message to Maria personally.

"Will you stay over?" Motte called after him.

"It'll be a day-long journey on horseback. Yes, I'll stay over."

Now that Joseph had been admitted to the bar a free man, he had become politically active. Traveling on horseback suited him well. For he, and other young hotheads thirsting to take a hand in shaping the new constitution, tired of the British legacy of public administration perpetuated by their elders long after independence, were holding rallies at wayside taverns throughout the country to air their discontent.

Ordinarily, Joseph would have been hotly campaigning as he rode the dust-laden King's highway to Dean Hall Plantation, but today his thoughts were of Maria and his contempt for the man who had deserted her. The letter he carried invited Maria to spend the summer with the family in Charleston, and involuntarily, his mind turned to Piers. It had come as a surprise that his father had kept Piers on after the escapade with Maria. Friends said Piers should have been dismissed. However, his father had seemed satisfied with the duel, that scores had been settled by the duel, and said that he had no quarrel with Piers. Joseph thought his father had been influenced by Algie and John Ashe, especially John Ashe. John Ashe admired Piers, and spent many hours in his company reading poetry and studying the natural flora down by the riverside. "John Ashe is not like the rest of us," Joseph was thinking. Now, Nisbet was a man of the world; he contrasted them. Riding the solitary highway, he returned his mind to his first meeting with the gentleman, the stupendous wedding breakfast in glittering New York, the support of Maria's wonderful theatrical friends, the incredibly aged Bella holding court, his own shy advances to pretty Fanny, and Maria's radiant happiness.

Chapter Sixteen

Joseph brought the news personally during a business trip to New York. "Lady Nisbet has a fine boy and is impatient for her knight's arrival." He observed the gentleman's lowered gaze to be the stoop of age, the hump back, the stringy silvery hair, wrinkled forehead, scaly beak nose. "My sister is most anxious," he continued. "She has received no word from her husband and fears for his safety."

"My great-nephew writes to no one," came the terse reply. "She had a fine boy, you say? That is good news."

"But the trip to Scotland," Joseph persisted. "We understand you were aware of Sir John's intentions. My sister pleaded with him to delay. He refused her and insisted upon an immediate sailing, because of the entail, he told her."

"Ah, the entail! Please be seated my dear sir. I fear my great-nephew is an incurable reprobate. What I have to tell you will shock you as much as it has shocked me." The frail old man, seated himself carefully, brought his stick between his knees, placed his hands over it to rest his chin upon them. With pale, watery eyes he scrutinized Joseph, whom he had not met before. At length he said, "Sir John's rightful claim to the baronetcy was called into question."

"Is that so?" Joseph said dryly.

In a slow quavering voice the old gentleman began the saga of the succession. "Our family has suffered years of legal battle ever since Sir John's parents were lost off the Carolina coast. Cape Fear you know. It's devilishly treacherous."

"We understand he and his younger brother Alex were holidaying with you here in New York at the time of the tragedy."

"The poor orphans were in danger of being disinherited and declared bastards."

"Bastards!" Joseph cried.

"The Nisbets in Edinburgh had no proof of Sir John's marriage, the boys' father."

Joseph relaxed. "Like father, like son," he said as his eyes laughed.

The old gentleman was not amused. "They had their Swiss valet scour the French countryside for traces of the girl's connections," he went on.

"Claudine Fauve, she was born. She and the boys' father lived together in France for several years, but no proof of their having been married there could be found."

"How was the legitimacy finally resolved?"

"Only last year, unanimously by the Lords of Session, in favor of the Nisbets. My evidence was the only proof."

"So, Sir John's heir in entail is secure. Their baby son is next heir in entail. His trip to Scotland is quite unnecessary at this time. Lady Nisbet called in Dr. Murray. He insisted she should not travel till after the birth."

"My great-nephew has not visited the family for ten years. I advised him to carry Lady Nisbet with him, and go by a Glasgow or Leith ship to avoid the enemy in the Channel. Alas! Had he but taken my advice." The old gentleman's face sagged despondently. Joseph felt there was something he was hiding.

"You have news of Sir John?" he hazarded.

"I have distressing news, sir. My Edinburgh cousins are much displeased with him. They write he dashes away at London, Bath, et cetera, makes merry with his wife as young folks will, and comes not near his estates."

"Wife!" Joseph sprang to his feet.

"The poor dears, they are deceived."

"Whatever shall I tell Maria!"

· · · · ·

When Victor Deas learned that Sir John Nisbet had married one of the Waccamaw Alstons, he felt violently antagonistic. He called to mind the notoriously self-confident and arrogant family patriarch. Any Alston interference in the running of Dean Hall rice plantation he would resist with every means he knew how. This was his attitude when Lady Nisbet arrived at his Charleston countinghouse.

Victor Deas glanced at the pile of unanswered letters gathering dust on the shelf. Lately they were full of invective. The suspicions of the Nisbets in Scotland had been roused. No remittances had been received these ten years. But three thousand miles of Atlantic Ocean separated them from their property in land and Negroes.

Victor Deas had been both factor and manager ever since the plantation was restored to the Nisbets after the war. He could barely remember Sir John's grandfather, Alexander Nisbet. But old Humpy up at the plantation, who had come straight from Africa, knew him best. He knew how the white buckra could wield an ax to clear jungle as good as any man. "Whew! He be a giant!" old Humpy would look skyward. "But he be good Maussa," Humpy would say waving a hand in the direction of the slave quarters which resembled an African village. "Dis land ours," he was fond of saying, "because we de firs' to clear de jungle." And Victor Deas was happy to leave it that way for he saw some truth in it. Without the Negroes not a grain of rice would ever reach the hungry European markets. He had salted away a tidy sum himself, taking his commission on the sales and pocketing "the petty cash", as he called the surplus after deducting the expenses—supplying the plantation implements, hand hoes and the like, and the slaves' subsistence.

But, sitting opulently now behind his large, mahogany desk fingering the gold watch chain stretched across his embroidered waistcoat, he was anything but happy. He knew a few plantation mistresses reputed to be ogresses. His imagined picture of Lady Nisbet was not flattering. He took a pinch of snuff to soothe himself and gave the order for Lady Nisbet to be announced.

⋅ ⋅ ⋅ ⋅ ⋅

Maria entered with aplomb, her dress a startling emerald silk charmeuse, her parasol a sword, her fiery dark eyes ready for battle. Victor Deas lost the monocle from his right eye. He had expected a martinet. He was confronted with a goddess. Suddenly Maria dissolved into peals of laughter.

Victor Deas drew a large handkerchief from his vest pocket, and wiped the sweat dripping into his beard. "You find me amusing, Ma'am?"

"Why, no, Mr. Deas. I have not made an entrance for quite a while. I simply enjoyed the effect."

Victor Deas did not understand. "If I have been discourteous I beg your forgiveness Ma'am." After composing himself he said, "You have a matter you wish to discuss?"

Maria leaned confidentially toward him, a scent of fresh gardenias wafting upon the air. "I believe I am the victim of a conspiracy of silence," she said dramatically.

"Ma'am?"

"I think I shall die if Sir John does not return soon!"

"Ireland's in revolt, and the French are poised to invade Britain," said Deas. "Everything's in turmoil." But then he remembered something. In the taverns on the dockside where factors woo ships' captains for space for rice destined for Europe, he had heard a rumor Nisbet was seen with an Italian prima donna. At the time, he thought nothing of it. "Pray God she does not discover," he thought now.

"He is long overdue," Maria said. She erected a barrier of wrath to hide her terrible fear of losing him.

"They say the British navy is mutinous. I expect Sir John is having difficulty getting a passage."

"Shucks! Mr. Deas," Maria flung a contemptuous oath, driving the point of her parasol viciously into the floorboards. "Tell me how many ships have crossed the ocean since he left on his short trip?" she said emphasizing the briefness with sarcasm.

"If I hear any news..." Victor Deas began nervously.

"I am returning to my family until Sir John arrives."

"But you are plantation mistress!" he said unbelieving.

"What a silly notion. They have been without a plantation mistress for years. I am a stranger in my own home!"

"A stranger, Ma'am?"

"A stranger, Mr. Deas. Oh yes, the Negroes are docile, but their faces are masks."

Victor Deas had not thought of it as lonely. During his rare visits to the plantation, arriving as he usually did at harvest when there was feasting and dancing, he was received by chanting crowds. For years he had traded on Sir John's pioneering grandfather's special relationship with the Negroes. A Scottish chief, Alexander Nisbet selected only tall races direct from Africa, especially Mundingoes whose tribal affiliations he likened to those of his own clansmen.

Neighboring planters thought him mad with his "village", a replica of an African village, his Negroes had extended family kinship ties, control vested in a council of elders, and no driver to whip up the slaves on task work. As he always answered, it is the Negroes who know how to prepare the land for planting, first burning off trash, leaping from the fire, beating back the flames when the wind shifts unexpectedly, chopping up the clayey tidal swamps with angled hoes on long springy handles, planting, flooding the bunded plats, weeding, draining off the water, and cutting the ripened rice stalks, head by head, with amazing dexterity.

"They've no option, Ma'am, but to accept you. They have nowhere to run," said Victor Deas.

Maria struck a melodramatic attitude. "The house is dead! We will stay with my father till Sir John returns. My baby will have other children to play with and loving nursemaids."

Victor Deas cloaked his relief. Years of indolence had made him resentful of change, but this was not the most staggering revelation of the afternoon.

"And I shall go back on the stage!" Maria said.

Chapter Seventeen

There was no outward evidence at the daily ritual of family gatherings for dinner that anything was amiss. But the waiting, all the irritations of Clifton in the tropical heat, was driving Maria to desperation. She longed to share little John with his father. Instead, she shared him with her teenage sister, Charlotte, who had become mildly possessive in her new role as aunt.

To Maria, so far from Europe, rumors of Napoleon's war being waged with emotional ferocity across continental frontiers, Britain left without allies, a mutinous navy, a brutalized army, and French invasions imminent, had the unreality of fiction. So long as European ports remained open to shipments of Carolina rice, the wars in Europe were not taken seriously. But one horrifying, recurring dream, that her husband had been coaxed into bearing arms for his king and country, tormented Maria.

"It's monstrous, I know," she told Joseph.

"Completely out of character," Joseph said. "He's delayed Maria, delayed by the troubles."

"But why does he not write?" Maria exploded.

"Like his great uncle said, he writes to no one."

But her dream would not go away. She became more and more irritable at the bustle of plantation life which spared no time for her phobias. If only Papa too had laid the guilt upon her of a neglected wife she had so dramatically rejected in the parlors of the grandames of Charleston last summer. Oh God! "We're family," she fancied him thinking. "My wandering daughter has returned." He's never going to accept John. "But little John is an Alston," she could hear him saying. She wanted to scream at his assumption of ownership.

Joseph had gone north again to join a political rally. She felt trapped and caged.

• • • • •

It was an idle boast of Algernon's, "I'm the first real American in our family." It was one of those arguments the brothers fell into with Piers about the patriots, about the revolution, even about the blood and thunder a hundred years before independence from the time the first Alston came over from London to settle in Carolina.

Piers was in a provocative mood. "American? What is an American?" He and the brothers had set off for the wild jungles of Bull Creek on a hunting expedition. Sleeping under the stars they could hardly see through the dense canopy of foliage. They had roasted a bush pig, and well-sated, were keeping the fire alive to ward off marauding animals.

"Hang on, Piers. We've all been born and bred here, and we've fought hard for what is rightly ours."

"Citizenship, that's what you're talking about. We're still shackled with one of Britain's worst legacies, a line of disparate peoples strung out in isolated provinces the whole way down the Atlantic coast."

"Traditionally jealous. Cut off from one another by bush paths, dirt tracks, alien ideologies," John Ashe said. "Don't you feel alien, Piers?"

The firelight flickered across the brothers' faces. Piers turned his gaze from one to the other. Algie's face had an alert expression. He was red-necked, like some pinelands overseer, from long hours spent on his father's plantations. He loved the culture so much so that rice almost sprouted from his ears. John Ashe, on the other hand, was sensitive, aesthetic-looking. He was no rustic planter's boy; his intimate relationship with Piers, a fearfully guarded secret. It was a loaded question, and Piers answered it with a quotation from Edward Young's Night Thoughts on Life, Death, and Immortality.

" 'We cut our cable, launch into the world,
    And fondly dream each wind and star our friend.' "

"So you do feel alien among our southern belles, you cryptic, Connecticut Yankee," Algie said. "Why do you stay?"

"It's true. We Yankees from Connecticut do reject any idea of union. We've made our fortunes trading rum and iron bars for African men and women, selling to the Caribbean islands. Greedy merchants, fighting men, but I've no stomach for it."

Algie drew a wad of tobacco from a metal container, and began stuffing it into a clay pipe. "Danny Haggar still bears you malice."

"A duel's a duel," John Ashe said with an air of finality. He moved from the fire into the shadows, and rolled himself in a blanket. After a while, Piers joined him. Piers was glad Maria had left Clifton. He was no longer in the wrath of love, but she was all made of passion.

• • • • •

It was the surprise letter from Fanny that decided Maria. "You'll never guess darling. I'm here in Philadelphia! I've joined Tom Wignell's troupe at the Chestnut. Poor Willy Dunlap—he's quite lost control at the Park. You wouldn't believe the bickerings, the jealousies. He's getting no help from Johnny Hodgkinson either. Terribly sad. Lottie's fallen ill. They say it's consumption. She's such a wonderful actress, such a lovely person. Johnny's heartbroken. Can't you get that charming husband of yours to bring you on a visit to Philadelphia? It's pure magic! Oh my! When I first saw the gigantic Liberty Bell way up there in the belfry of Independence Hall. Felt goosey all over with pride. Every American should make this pilgrimage. Anyway, you'll rave over the Chestnut Street Theatre darling. We're putting on *The Contrast*."

In her agony of waiting, Maria was convinced the letter was from her husband and the rage she had cultivated with so much love at his continual silence faded away. But when she opened it the shock of disappointment brought her to the verge of tears. No power on earth seemed able to raise her from her prostration, then Motte came into the room, excited, and asked about the letter.

"It's from Fanny," Maria masked her distress. She moved across the room, stared from the window beyond the slave cabins across empty lands. Their harvest yielded up a feast of trash for alligators and other reptiles wallowing in the muddy banks. "She's in Philadelphia and invites us over," she said in a flat voice.

"Oh, my dear!" Motte said as she reached out to console her.

● ● ● ● ●

With Charleston hardly emerged from a ban on theatrical productions, the stigma upon actors as vagrants, and the Dock Street Theatre burned down yet again, musical recitals were now the rave. Maria had found few sympathetic ears in her battle for a revival of the drama. It had simply inspired hostility when she talked openly of the debt the new American drama owed to the English stage. She could not withdraw her mind from the play which opened the original Dock Street Theatre forty years before the War of Independence, Farquhar's *The Recruiting Officer*. Her chance discovery of the play in a dusty corner of a Charleston bookstore had so dazzlingly fit her mood.

It was not the stage history of this lively comedy of loving and fighting that excited her. The play's initial production was almost a century ago at the Drury Lane Theatre in London, with grudging comments upon its broad humor. Also mundane to her was the attitude of post-revolutionary actor-managers who excluded the play from their repertoires. It was Farquhar's placing his play in a town like Shrewsbury, and drawing his characters from real life Britons, that fired her imagination. For she desperately wanted to identify with her adored husband's country, to find an affinity with John out there. But instead the play had left her badly shaken, her mind obsessively fixed on the marriage stakes transformed by wealth, and Captain Plume the recruiting officer's boast: "I am not that rake the world imagines."

Chapter Eighteen

Hearing of Maria's new stage appearance at the Chestnut and having something important to tell her, Joseph had stopped over in Philadelphia. He was on his way back to New York after campaigning in the Carolinas, during which he had been the cause of another painful rift at Clifton. His father discovered that Joseph was fighting for Aaron Burr and not for Thomas Jefferson as he was doing. "Burr captures the aspirations of us young Americans," Joseph told Maria. "Pa's friends are for Thomas Jefferson. He's just another stiff-necked Virginian. Burr's the man of the moment."

"But they are both Democratic-Republicans," Maria interjected, "and besides, Jefferson's an old-timer."

"True enough. Both are in the same fight against the Federalists, but Burr's magnetism will secure him the presidency, mark my words. Still, I didn't come here to talk politics."

"Let me guess. Papa has asked you to persuade me to go home."

"Of course!" Joseph laughed lightly.

"And how's my little Johnny?"

"Thriving, Maria. He's a real charmer. Don't stay away too long, Maria."

"He's safe with Mauma. I'll fetch him after the theatre season. and take our little boy to the sea islands. We'll make sandcastles till his father comes home." Suddenly Maria flung her arms about Joseph. "I'm beginning to despair of ever seeing John again. The stage is my lifeline. I can't go back to Clifton. I only meant to visit, but Tom Wignell's troupe has given me such a wonderful welcome here."

"And you have Fanny."

"She's wonderful. She hasn't changed a bit and is longing to see you. I do believe she's in love with you."

Joseph lowered his eyes. It had been a chance encounter running into Fanny at the Chestnut Street Theatre. He had arrived in Philadelphia travel stained. He had taken an early tub and gone to a show. She had just arrived from New York and was lonely. He had invited her to dine at one of Philadelphia's most exclusive taverns. There they had relived good times at the Park, at Ma'am Schroeder's hostelry, with Johnny Hodgkinson's magnificent troupe, and they had gone on drinking. If only they had not made love. He wondered what he would feel meeting Fanny again. But, he was quite resolved. "There's nothing between us," he answered Maria's unspoken question.

"I don't believe it," her dark eyes flashed. "You shy brother of mine, you couldn't take your eyes off her when I introduced you in New York. Marry Fanny, Joseph."

Had Fanny confided in Maria? He felt embarrassed. "That's what I came to tell you. I'm engaged to be married to Theodosia Burr."

* * * * *

Shock at Joseph's news stayed with Maria for several days. She remembered seeing Theodosia Burr only once, a glittering New York beauty chaperoned by her father. Young officers in the auditorium dazzled by her, seated, bejeweled, coquettishly fanning herself, in a box normally reserved for high dignitaries. It was the night Mr. Hamilton came to see the play, *André*. The entire cast had been nervous at what he would write in the *New York Evening Post*. Watching from the wings, one could not escape the rivalry between the two giants, Mr. Hamilton and Mr. Burr. Maria recalled the *New York Evening Post* made no mention of the Burrs.

She had not expected Fanny's violent reaction when she told her Joseph's news. "What a fate to be married to your boorish brother!"

"Oh, my dearling, you really do love him," Maria put a sympathetic arm around her.

"Marked for destruction!" Fanny exclaimed as she freed herself, striking an attitude from the Chestnut Street Theatre's current production of Willy Dunlap's play, *The Fatal Deception.* Fanny could trace her family's settlement in New England back to the arrival of the *Mayflower* nearly two centuries ago. Today, her people still lived on the bread line, her father scraped a living as a New York entertainer. She had not been so successful as Maria on the stage. She lived on her nerves, fearful of being laid-off. In her mind, the difference between them was Maria's security, her safety net, the opulent planter society of her birth.

Joseph had come into her life like a gift from God. The whole day long she wove fantasies of a loving home where her children would grow up never wanting. Joseph had spoken affectionately of his Waccamaw plantation, his intention of settling down when the election was over. She had read into his open invitation, a proposal. Now, in one terrible blow, all her dreams were scattered to the wild winds. Her heart was ringed with ice.

To Maria, Fanny's expression was inscrutable. For the first time Fanny's auburn hair reminded her of that rebellious red streak in Joseph's own whenever the sunlight caught it; all at once, she felt hostile toward Fanny in Joseph's defense. "He's a ruthlessly ambitious politician," she said. "And Theodosia Burr moves in high society. They are well suited. Joseph says he's the luckiest man in the world."

"She won't survive your southern ways, or your steamy climate, the spoilt little Manhattan seventeen-year-old dearling of her Pa," Fanny said bitterly.

"She'll want for nothing. Joseph is a rich man."

"Mr. Burr's political rivals call him an unscrupulous rascal near to bankruptcy," Fanny mocked. "You only have to read the newspapers. You know what I think? He's sold his daughter."

"That's a wicked thing to say Fanny. I won't listen!" Maria clasped her hands over her ears striking an attitude of moral indignation.

♦ ♦ ♦ ♦ ♦

How would the people vote in the elections for president? Would they vote for him? Aaron Burr knew in the deep south everything depended on the way the Carolinas cast their vote. In South Carolina, you could count the powerful families on one hand—especially the Alstons and Allstons of Waccamaw. He knew their leanings. He knew that William Alston of Clifton was for Jefferson. He had to lure Joseph Alston to campaign for the "Burr ticket" with all the passion of a woman in love. He had to harness to himself the fellow's political sagacity and considerable wealth. For this, he was prepared to offer the one gift in his power, the hand of his daughter.

Nothing of his host's intentions did Joseph suspect when he arrived at the luxurious Manhattan mansion to celebrate Aaron Burr's victory over Alexander Hamilton for New York City. Finding himself among eminent politicians and their spouses, out-of-place among elegant New Yorkers, he looked desperately around for someone he knew. A large heavily-gilded punch bowl circulated in his direction, carried by a dandily-dressed black house servant. Nervously, he stretched out his hand but was instantly checked by a purposeful tap on the shoulder.

"May I present you to my daughter, Miss Burr?" Theodosia gave a polite curtsy, somewhat surprised at her father's special cordiality.

Joseph bowed stiffly. "'Tis a pleasure ma'am," he responded in his slurred southern drawl.

"Welcome to Richmond Hill," Theodosia said, vaguely recalling having seen him once before, the bearded face and short black curls with a streak of red. She then turned back to the group behind her, eager to join their chatter.

"Theodosia!"

She reeled at her father's displeasure.

"Mr. Alston would like to be appraised of the balls and the theatrical performances presently in town. He will lead you in to dinner."

Joseph stood completely bewildered. He knew he was not the guest of honor. He thought this most beautiful girl in the whole of New York looked shattered, but she said nothing. Obediently, she slipped her hand through his arm.

• • • • •

Theodosia Burr, who could not remember her deceased mother, idolized her father; not for a moment would she wish to cause him the slightest displeasure. Yet, as the sumptuous meal proceeded, perfected by the superb quality of the French clarets from the Burr cellars, she found increasing difficulty in drawing Joseph into the conversation, in understanding the unfamiliar southern accent, and politely trying to help him over his stammer as his discomfort became more pronounced. Her attention wandered when she found him no scholar, no wit either, and quite lacking in charm. Bewilderment clouded his face as the distinguished New Yorkers around him conversed now in English, now in French.

Suddenly, Theodosia was aware of a scolding look in her father's piercing black eyes from the far end of the table. Instantly, fearful of his displeasure, she turned the conversation into an inquiry after the pleasures of Carolinian society, so different from theirs she supposed, leaning toward Joseph with an air of innocent curiosity.

The muscles of Joseph's face relaxed. Of the rice swamps he could speak with confidence, and of race week, and of the popularity of music and the drama, oblivious of the bored inattention of his neighbors.

But her father would not release Theodosia from her duty as hostess till, mercifully, it was time for the servants to clear the dishes, bring fruit and nuts to be taken with a pinch of snuff, and a clean wine glass for the Madeira.

Theodosia rose, signaling the retirement of the ladies.

• • • • •

Joseph had tumbled into the glamorous company of the New Yorker Theodosia Burr, but theirs was not the mad, whirlwind romance he had enjoyed with Fanny. As he struggled to keep up with the bright, young people who kept company with Theodosia, his downtrodden look earned him the unhappy title of buffoon. Aaron Burr had rushed him into a proposal of marriage he instinctively knew Theodosia had tearfully resisted. She openly showed distaste for his southern ways, but finally capitulated, not out of love for him, but under pressure from her adored father. Joseph felt a sharp pain of loneliness and bewilderment whenever she shrank from his touch.

He took refuge behind his public image. His speeches were skillful. There was a mastery of his subject that gripped his audience, and his hot canvassing for the "Burr ticket" bit hard into the Federalist camp, especially infuriating the Carolinians who complained that the arrogant young Alston was swinging so many of their sons to the Republican cause. If voting were to be by a single majority of the one hundred and six members of the House of Representatives, Joseph had no doubt that the result would favor Burr. Sixteen states each would have a single vote.

Joseph acted like a crazy man. He withdrew huge sums from The Oaks plantation to meet the prodigious costs of his future father-in-law's campaign. "Burr for President! Burr for President!" Three words that seared his brain by day and through hot sleepless nights.

* * * * *

At last, the body of elders was gathered in the Hall of Representatives, every member dragged along, the sick, the seriously ill for whom sofas and nursing attendance were provided. On the first ballot, eight states voted for Jefferson, six for Burr, with Vermont and Maryland equally divided between them. Hurried attempts to sway the two small states only added confusion as each new ballot gave the same result—eight for Jefferson, six for Burr, with the remaining two continuing undecided.

All night they voted, into the next morning, twenty-nine ballots without the slightest change by noon. Never had Joseph's nerves been so ragged. He marveled at Aaron Burr's exuberant confidence, tireless after hours of waiting, as the voting elders visibly wearied at the determination of the House not to adjourn until a choice had been made between Jefferson and Burr. It was no use. The two undecided could not decide. From sheer exhaustion, the House took a recess.

Chapter Nineteen

When Victor Deas called her to his countinghouse, Maria felt a shiver of fear up her spine. The imperativeness of his letter convinced her the news was bad. She traveled the long land journey from Philadelphia to Charleston, desperate for it to end. She had impatiently strutted tavern forecourts at stopovers waiting for the unhurried gossiping mail coach to proceed to its next staging post. When she finally reached Charleston, she donned the same emerald silk charmeuse she had worn at her first meeting with Mr. Deas, as if it were a talisman.

Her unceremonious burst into his office sent him into a flummox. He was recovering from a weakening attack of the dreaded swamp fever, and she appeared before him like an apparition. She rudely brought him to his senses with the shrillness of her voice, her hands clutching the edge of his desk. "You asked for me!"

Clumsily, he scraped back his fine leather chair, and stretched out a puffy damp hand. "I beg your indulgence, Ma'am. You have arrived unannounced. It is an impertinence. I shall demand an apology."

But Maria was not on her dignity. She had swept his minions aside to enter his office. "Don't keep me in suspense!" she cried.

"Dear me," Victor Deas said as he fumbled among his papers. "Yes, here it is, a letter from Sir John."

But when he laid it before her, she made no attempt to pick it up.

"Will you not open it, Ma'am?"

· · · · ·

Fearful of what she might learn, Maria waited till she was closeted in her boudoir before opening the letter.

> "Now, you must not be jealous dearest girl, I have
> not slipped back to my old habits..."

Maria gave a jubilant shout, and laughed into the mirror. It was more than she had dared to hope. She began to hallucinate. There, reflected, she saw her beloved John approaching, his sensuous lips parted. She felt the blood pounding through her veins, her brain tricked into a phantom passion sharing a joyous bed. She let the bewitching moment linger, long after the hallucination, before she read further.

> "If you could see that wretched land. Britain is fighting a military genius. Napoleon is preparing to invade from the north coast of France. My old Regiment, the 59th, has requested my recall. Army recruiting officers are swarming into the English countryside grabbing every male they can lay hands on. But here I am, my beauty, cleverly escaped to Italy. How long have we been apart? Does my son have a picture of his father? As soon as it is safe, dear girl, I shall set sail."

Slowly she folded the letter, covered it with kisses. "Oh my love, my dearling love!" she cried aloud, clasping the letter to her chest, tears filling her eyes. "Come quickly, my love! Come quickly!"

• • • • •

On their way south, Joseph and Theodosia stopped over in Washington to witness Thomas Jefferson's inauguration. How nearly it had been Aaron Burr's; how nearly Theodosia had been First Lady. Joseph thought back over that agonizing election.

Aaron had been in high spirits after the recess and had spent the night using every trick of his fertile brain to turn the friends of Jefferson to his own cause. As the new day dawned, he had left jauntily for the House of Representatives, confident of victory. But the thirtieth ballot was taken with precisely the same result as the previous night. Tensions grew as Aaron's followers knew only too well that Jefferson needed but a single state vote—either that of Vermont or of Maryland—and the controversy would be at an end.

After the thirty-fifth ballot with no change, pandemonium broke out. Some angrily cried that they would rather go without a president than have Jefferson elected, but others, utterly weary of the contest and all the intrigue which it was generating, aimed to put a stop to it once and for all at the next ballot.

While Aaron was elsewhere engaged in heated discussion, Jefferson made a secret pact with his closest friends. These he authorized to say that if he were elected no change would be made relating to commerce, the navy, or the public debt, and that subordinate officers would neither be removed on account of their political character, nor have complaints against their conduct.

Joseph could not get out of his head the awful drumming of fingers upon the bench, the only sound in the charged atmosphere as the thirty-sixth ballot was taken. Suddenly, it was all over. There was a roar of applause: "Jefferson for president! Burr for vice president" The member from Vermont, who held the divided vote of that state, had absented himself, and two of Maryland's four members had voted blank.

"We have overturned the Federalists, truly a good omen for the beginning of the new century," Joseph had nervously tried to placate Aaron, only to be heatedly reminded that the outgoing president had been Washington's vice president. "Jefferson shall not serve a second term!" Aaron had stormed. "There is a precedent for my becoming president!"

But Theodosia's thoughts were far from those of Joseph's. On the second day of February, only four weeks earlier, she and Joseph had stood dazed before the Reverend Mr. Johnson in an anteroom of the Albany Chambers that her father had secured for the occasion; they had solemnly enunciated the marriage vows. The tie-vote controversy was still raging, and friends of Jefferson immediately threw suspicion upon the unlikely union between the brilliant and beautiful New Yorker and the wealthy southerner. Aaron appeared blandly indifferent to the buzz of conjecture about his ears, and with the ceremony over, the couple took tea with the hurriedly assembled guests.

"Do you not think I should stay by your side?" Theodosia had pleaded. "Mr. Jefferson's tactic was a most cruel device."

"Dear me, no my child," Aaron had taken her into his embrace.

"But Papa, Mr. Alston is so young. Besides, I have no desire to leave you for that unwholesome Carolina climate."

"Mr. Alston's age is of no consequence, dear child," he had replied. "We are not Carolinians. We do not disapprove of early marriages. Neither will the climate affect you for you will be of rich estate and suitably protected."

Then he had hesitated, and she desperately hoped her adored Papa was relenting. But when he spoke again, she knew she had been deceived.

"You see, my child, I must have access to the Alston wealth to guarantee my political future, so I wish you to marry Mr. Alston without delay."

In his voice was that warning note she never dared defy. She had brushed away a tear to put on a brave face.

Chapter Twenty

When Maria arrived at Clifton for the family gathering she was still suffering nervous exhaustion from unfounded fears of bad news. How many Charleston families had waited in vain for loved ones who had braved the treacherous crossing? Maria's dreams were nightmares of great walls of water hurtling toward the summer islands, smashing houses, and the seabed strewn with ships crushed in the hungry jaws of the voracious Atlantic Ocean. One recurring nightmare saw her beloved husband among the dead bones and lost riches of centuries of wrecks in swirling sands fathoms deep. However, her relief that John was safe in Italy was turning to frustrated anger. She had written to him that little Johnny would soon be three and that he longed to see his father. Besides, she hated being a grass widow, and she hated her father's attitude. His displeasure at the imminent arrival of a Yankee into the family circle exceeded even his outrage at having to accept John Nisbet as a son-in-law, a man with no riband to mark him a patriot.

"Where do you two rebel children of my poor lamented first wife think your great love affairs will end?" he raged as the house servants scurried about with preparations for the welcoming party. But, Maria's was a resentment that boded ill for the new wife. She had not forgiven Joseph for jilting Fanny.

As Joseph and Theodosia's arrival drew near, the family atmosphere became fractious. Motte took to her bed claiming early labor pains with her seventh child on the way and left Maria to welcome the eagerly inquisitive Brookgreen cousins of the double 'l' Allston branch of the family.

* * * * *

As her tired eyes fell upon the large gathering in front of the grand colonnaded southern plantation house, flight was all Theodosia could think of, flight back to her father. She could have wept, but he would have scolded her. She descended from the Alston chaise tired, wretched, and travel stained after the sixteen day journey from Washington on rough roads in bumping coaches. Bad nights in dirty taverns had taken their toll and she had turned to Joseph for support. But Joseph was greeting his father, forgetting her misery.

Maria stepped forward gratified that she had the advantage of height. "I am Lady Nisbet, your sister-in-law," she said adopting an attitude of grandeur, "and this is my son John." She pushed him fondly to the front.

Hardly had Theodosia registered Maria's antagonism when Joseph's father took over the introductions with an aloofness which caused her spirits to sink even further. "These are my children by my poor lamented first wife. I am told my daughter, Lady Nisbet, has some claim to fame on the New York stage," he said giving a casual wave of the hand. "No doubt you have seen her treading the boards. You will find the attitude of our southern plantocracy opposed to theatrical ventures. And these are my sons, William Algernon and John Ashe," he said.

The boys bowed stiffly as Algie cast an interested eye at Theodosia's high-waisted bosom. "Just like the saucy boys back home," she thought as she managed a smile. She was about to remark how John Ashe reminded her of a literary friend when a bouncy, eager-faced schoolgirl peered at her from behind the brothers and giggled nervously.

"Don't be silly, Charlotte," Maria rebuked. "Come out and say hello."

"And these are my children by my dear wife, Mrs. Alston, whom you will meet later," William Alston went on. "She has taken to her bed. Just a little indisposed," he dismissed Theodosia's inquiring look and began naming her children by pointing an elegant finger. "Rebecca, Thomas Pinckney, Charles, Jacob Motte." Theodosia looked wearily at the upturned solemn little faces, their hands clinging tightly to the apron strings of a fat beaming Negress cradling baby Elizabeth. She especially noticed Rebecca, who stared with unblinking eyes which made her feel uncomfortable.

Suddenly she cried out, "Am I not to be allowed the privacy of a change of clothing, a tub to dip into?" But her father-in-law had begun a new round of introductions of cousins, aunts, neighbors, sending her dizzy and sick with names and faces she could not possibly remember. Mercifully, someone called in a booming voice, "Is it not time for a celebratory drink, William? A lime punch would you say."

◆ ◆ ◆ ◆ ◆

When Joseph found Theodosia sobbing into her pillow, he was visibly distressed. "Why, Theo, my dearest," he lifted her gently. "Whatever has upset you? The family is pleased with you."

She wanted to tell him she felt desperately lonely. She wanted to tell him she felt suffocated by the heat, nauseated by the smells rising from the swamps, frightened by unnerving screeches of wild animals in the fringing foliage. On the journey, he had spoken excitedly of his plans to make The

Oaks habitable. He talked of his boyhood at the plantation when Grandpa Joseph was alive, of wild romps with Maria on their Indian ponies, and of Grandpa Joseph calling them his "little freedom fighters". Were all those people she had been presented to earlier patriot Allstons of the double "l" branch from Brookgreen plantation? "They will be our neighbors," Joseph had said. But he had not taken her straight to The Oaks as she expected, and this had upset her. But she said nothing about it now, just nestled gratefully against his shoulder.

"Come, dear girl," he roused her. "'Tis nearly time for dinner and you are not yet changed." He clapped his hands, and his body servant appeared.

"I ordered a maid for the mistress. Who is it?" he said

"'Tis Emma, Maussa. Dey say sh'um be de sma'tes gal in de quarters," said his body servant.

"Bring her here," commanded Joseph.

A slim, black wench entered, her crinkly hair immaculately plaited over her shapely head, her cotton dress sparkling white against her dark skin.

Theodosia cheered up. The girl looked clean and neat. In her father's house she had a French maid. "I'll soon teach black Emma how to be a good lady's maid," she thought to herself, surprised only that the girl kept her eyes permanently lowered.

But throughout her first night on the Waccamaw, Theodosia could not shake off a sense of foreboding.

Chapter Twenty-One

It was at the St. Cecilia Ball in Charleston last January that Sarah McPherson fell blindly into love. Ever since her father died of cholera, fear of a cholera epidemic on their modest plantation became an obsession for her mother, the horror of it driving her into an hysteria of sanitary vigor, so that the lightening of her daughter's love for the eligible young John Ashe was like a victory. She had prayed for a suitor from one of the leading Santee families before a case of cholera occurred among the black servants in their slave quarters. Shaken by the conviction that God was present, she welcomed the union with tears streaming down her face. Never in her wildest dreams had she imagined an alignment with the fabulously wealthy Alstons of Waccamaw.

John Ashe Alston had shown little interest in girls and had shrugged off his flirtatious party-loving kid brother, Algernon's sly asides upon his friendship with Piers. So, when he was struck by Sarah McPherson's impassioned seduction, he was emotionally unprepared.

"Marry the girl, damn you!" said his father. "Comes of a good southern family. She'll make a fine plantation mistress, and bear you many children."

* * * * *

Joseph shaded his eyes, looked across the rice plats to the muddy Waccamaw River beyond. The plantation was a wedding present from his father, and he had tenanted it to Sarah and John Ashe, not expecting to live on it himself. He should have told Theodosia. He should never have let her believe they could move into The Oaks straight-away. It was sheer folly taking for granted she would fit in at Clifton till he came into full possession of The Oaks. He cursed the stringency of the law in the handling of wills. Early death was not uncommon in these unhealthy swamps, and so often the wishes of the deceased did nothing but tear families apart. Grandpa Joseph would rise in his grave if he knew the storm over his will. "Goddamn it!" he would have said. "Let the boy take possession now. How could I know he would marry young?"

John Ashe cut into his train of thought. "What's the history of this place?"

"Pa bought it from Anthony Pawley. Since Pa already owns Weehawka."

"He's kicked the last Pawley off the Neck," John Ashe finished for Joseph.

"Weehawka?" Sarah looked puzzled.

John Ashe pointed across a rough road. "That, too, was a Pawley plantation. Pa never forgave their grandfather for being loyal to the British to his last breath. On Waccamaw, dear girl, the petty hatreds and feuds of the Revolutionary War will never die."

Sarah fixed her eye on a small house standing in solitary isolation a little way from the river. "Did the Pawleys live here?" she said doubtfully.

"Gracious no! Anthony has a thriving merchant house in Georgetown," said Joseph. "Probably left his overseer in the house."

"We've found it horribly neglected. I've had the carpenters working on it ever since we moved in," John Ashe said.

"And strangely," Joseph went on, "the plantation didn't have a name. It was simply registered to Anthony. Pa christened it Hagley. The day he bought the plantation he happened to be dining with friends just back from Europe. They were so thrilled with England, especially with their visit to Hagley Park. You know how Pa likes anything that sounds a bit grand."

"Well, there's nothing grand about these marshes. The plantation is too close to the river for my liking," said John Ashe.

"Powerful tides flood the rice plats down here. Good hunting grounds too."

Sarah had stopped listening. "Theodosia is miserable at Clifton," Joseph had said. "You won't mind if we share with you and John Ashe."

But she did mind.

◆ ◆ ◆ ◆ ◆

"The Hagley house is primitive," Theodosia began a letter to her father. "Oh Papa! I don't think I can bear it!" She leaned back in her chair to reflect upon her situation.

At Clifton there was no privacy; noisy children ran constantly in and out of her bedchamber uninvited; the house servants chatted away in that Gullah language of theirs which she could not understand and it got on her nerves. After the first flush of excitement at who she was, how she looked, and what her wardrobe contained, she found herself largely ignored by the family. As for Joseph's stepmother, Motte, Theodosia had decided she was a hopeless victim of narrow-minded polite society. Whatever Theodosia wanted to do, in Motte's little world, conventional rules of personal behavior did not permit in a married woman. She felt trapped and lonely with Joseph away most of the day, until she discovered he went riding with Maria. And then she just exploded. She ran from the house in her flimsy muslin without a wrap, and no straw hat upon her head against the burning tropical sun. Joseph was handing his horse to the stable boy. "How dare you go riding with Maria, and leave me penned up in this ugly prison."

Frantically looking left and right, he gripped her arms. "Theo," he said roughly. "Go inside. Everyone will hear you."

"What do I care?"

"Maria has problems. She wants my help."

"So have I. Take me away from here. Take me home."

All she could remember of the dreadful scene that followed was the hurt in Joseph's eyes. Poor Joseph. "What are we going to do?" she thought.

She took up her pen again. "My darling Papa, I beg you to let me travel north to visit my old home. I long to breathe the cool air, gaze upon the Hudson River flowing beneath Richmond Hill, pick you a large bowl of flowers of the sweetest perfume and the most astonishing colors. I'll be your 'Golden Thighs'," she said making flirtatious reference to the nineteen-year-old Abenaki Indian princess her father took with him on soldiering escapades long before he met her mother. "And we'll dine alone, and talk, and talk, and talk."

* * * * *

Joseph was in a desultory mood. Riding back to Hagley after seeing Theodosia off by fast packet to spend a few weeks with her father, he visualized the stately Richmond Hill Burr Mansion on Staten Island with its secluded groves and wealth of cedars looking down upon the Hudson. He thought with envy of the man who could make his Theodosia happy.

From early childhood, Joseph had been unsure of himself, a weakness he kept hidden behind a bearded face and an arrogant manner. Had he Aaron Burr's charm, his gift of a brilliant intellect, his magnetic personality, he could make Theodosia happy. The anguish of their honeymoon still haunted him — his blundering lovemaking. Aaron had bound Theodosia and himself together for life assuring them the character and habits of a twenty-two-year-old and a seventeen-year-old are not completely formed. They would grow together in mutual fondness. Something else troubled Joseph. Fanny had wordlessly, tearlessly clung to him with a desperation she could not disguise, when she learned of his engagement to Theodosia. He had pushed her away.

* * * * *

Sarah Alston was glad Theodosia had gone north to visit her father. They had been good friends at first, two vivacious teenage newlyweds giggling together, sharing secrets. It was the day John Ashe developed a touch of fever and Sarah insisted he stay indoors that things began to go wrong.

Joseph had gone out on the plantation. Despite his long absences campaigning for the Burr ticket, he could not kick the habit of rice culture. Hagley being wholly dependent on the efficiency of the tidal flow system, the rice plats had to be flooded and dried out regularly. Joseph knew it would have taken years of hard labor to clear this swamp of dense cypress trees and make use of the Waccamaw's tide water. In no time at all rats, alligators, and snakes had breached the banks. He had checked the "trunks", the floodgates with two facing doors set at intervals in the huge earth banks. Only the strongest Negroes were trunk-minders because of the heavy work of raising the outside door. Water from the river pushed open the inside door, filled the ditches around the fields, and flows over into the paddy rice plats. Again, the fields were drained, the trunk-minders lifted the inner door on an ebb tide, and the water leaving the rice plats forced open the outer door. Soon the new season's rice must be planted. Negro field workers had been busy for weeks chopping the clayey sods with their hoes and leveling the rice plats, while the trunk-minders got ready for the first flooding after the rice was planted, the sprout flow, so crucial for a good harvest.

From early morning Sarah herself had been supervising the work of the weavers and seamstresses, cutting out clothes for the slave children, still terribly excited by her new role as plantation mistress. She wanted to set up all the house servants and field slaves with new clothing to her own style. On her way back to the house she had delayed to sample the slave cook's freshly made loaf of cornbread and arranged for an extra allowance of molasses to be included in the slaves' ration. "Always err on the generous side," her mother had always taught her. Then she had raced back to the house bubbling with happiness, her long fair hair catching the gold-red lights of the setting sun. At first, she could not take it in. She rubbed her eyes as if waking from an unpleasant dream. Theodosia was reading aloud, with John Ashe's arm round her, and the words she caught made her choke, "...for love pursues an ever-devious race."

She caught John Ashe's eye bright with excitement. "You've been gone a long time my pretty little wife," he had sprung up.

"Well, you don't seem to have missed me," she had said coldly. He had pulled her into his arms and kissed her full on the mouth, but it had done nothing to ease her pang of jealousy. She could still hear Theodosia's teasing words.

"Why Sarah, I do believe you're upset! The poem needs to be read aloud. It's a powerful lament. Listen!"

But she would not bend. "The fever seems miraculously to have left you, John Ashe!" she had scoffed. That night they had their first row.

Chapter Twenty-Two

The rains were over. Everywhere there was a sense of relief. No hurricane had swept away the rice crop. The harvest was good, and with the sickly season over, plantation families had returned to their mansions, and had left behind deserted seashore summer houses and an uncanny quiet in Charleston's luxurious town dwellings that were evacuated till next year's February races.

Theodosia stayed at her father's Manhattan mansion the whole summer through, a thousand miles from Carolina's unhealthy marshes, while Maria languished at the Alston rambling sea island summer house on Sullivan's, off Charleston harbor, brooding upon her decision to quit Tom Wignell's Philadelphia troupe. "Little Johnny is still too young to have him without me," she had reasoned and decided to take a year off from acting. One day, idly watching her Johnny play with Motte's Jacob, happy as sand boys, she said, "Motte I think I have made a ghastly mistake."

Motte had safely delivered her seventh child and at thirty-two years had blossomed into a handsome society woman. William Alston had commissioned an artist to paint her portrait in the grand manner of his distinguished family name, a full-length masterpiece in ball dress—powdered wig to exquisite brocade gown which gave her superior stature and grace. What struck admirers of the portrait was the expression caught in the face by the artist's brush. What they saw was contentment. "'Tis shame, Maria, to waste young love apart," she had answered, her fingers nimbly shaping the tower of a sand castle to the delighted cries of her children.

"My Johnny and your Jacob are like twins. My heart is with the troupe. My little boy is happy with the family. I even envy Theodosia in New York," said Maria.

"You need to raise a family, twenty-three and still only one child. John Nisbet has deserted you too long," said Motte. Her tone was charitable, but Maria found it patronizing, and she tramped off in high dudgeon till she was quite alone. Then, facing the gray Atlantic, she vented her feelings. She screamed and screamed into the roar of the waves.

• • • • •

Johnny Nisbet had his mother's fiery dark eyes, a bright hyperactive child, slight in build with a pale oval-shaped face, and the same wild love of the theatrical. Each night he petitioned Maria to tell him another tale of the magical world of drama and, despite his tender years she took him to the new Charleston Theatre when Matthew Sully came to play harlequin. The atmosphere sent him breathless with excitement, throwing a lifeline to Maria's dejected spirits. She began weaving fantasies of Johnny, the boy-actor, starring with the greatest. For his third birthday in November at Clifton, she wrote a children's play. She called all the children in the neighborhood to act it, and the grown-ups to supply the audience.

One day, right out of the blue, when everyone was rushing around getting ready for Christmas Johnny suddenly said, "Mama, what's plat-eye?"

"Who's been telling you tales," she'd laughed dismissively, but it disturbed her. Mauma never spoke to the children about plat-eye. He must have heard one of the nursemaids threaten "plat-eye will get you" to silence an unruly child. The last thing she wanted was Johnny frightened by a malign spirit conjured up by one of her father's slaves. It was when sharing with Motte the task of handing out special Christmas rations of meat, molasses, salt, and rice to every working slave, that she fancied behind their inscrutable faces a scary world of slave beliefs. She mentioned it to Motte who looked anxious and said, "If you're sickening for the fever you should get straight to bed. I'll have Mauma bring you a dose of the bitter bark."

◆ ◆ ◆ ◆ ◆

Sarah and John Ashe arrived first.

"Have you heard the rumor, Maria?" Sarah said breathless with excitement. "Theodosia's very unhappy in her new home."

"Joseph spent all summer renovating The Oaks," said John Ashe. "Had a large extension built. We took a look while Joseph was in New York fetching Theodosia home."

"The roof's only half renewed. The other half is still untouched and rotten. Leaked buckets during the rains," said Sarah. "And no decent furniture, only two rickety rocking chairs on the verandah."

"I thought they would be staying over at your place again."

Maria caught a spiteful look in Sarah's eye. "I told Joseph our house is too small."

"And Theodosia absolutely refuses to come back here till her house is completed," John Ashe indicated the spaciousness of Clifton with an expansive wave of the hand.

Fanny's harsh comment upon Theodosia's father crossed Maria's mind. "He's sold his daughter." Then a thought occurred to her. After all there are two sides; Joseph has bought himself a political career—the vice president's son-in-law. For a brief moment, she felt almost sorry for Theodosia, caught in a tug-of-war between two aggressively ambitious men, but she said nothing. As soon as the couple arrived completing the family circle, William Alston of Clifton fired a musket by way of sending out Christmas greetings to their neighbors and a welcome to join in the feasting. Madrigal singers and minstrels began playing and singing the Yuletide favorites.

Maria, helped by her sister Charlotte, put the finishing touches to the simple decorations of foliage evergreens intertwined with fragrant winter honeysuckle. "Do you know what they call this on Waccamaw, Charlotte?" she said. "Kiss-me-at-the-gate."

Charlotte giggled, "I have no lover to kiss."

Oh, to be sixteen again, thought Maria admiring Charlotte's shining fair ringlets, large innocent blue eyes, trim chest and slender hips, so like the portrait hanging in the library of their long deceased mother. No wonder father spoils her. "Don't let your heart be broken, that's all," she said out loud.

◆ ◆ ◆ ◆ ◆

By the end of November, Theodosia knew that she was pregnant. But it was Joseph who broke the news to the family on Christmas morning. The slaves had received their Christmas day treat—a dram of rum, tobacco, and extra rations, and were frantically singing, dancing and drumming in front of the big house. Inside, after several punches, the family was on to the roast duck with southern spoon bread, when Joseph suddenly shouted, "Listen everyone! I'm to be a father!"

"Well! Well!" said Maria before the others could pull themselves out of their southern languor. "This calls for a toast. You must take plenty of exercise or you'll suffer, Theodosia." Maria fixed her eyes dotingly upon her Johnny. Theodosia flushed.

All eyes turned to the head of the table William Alston raised his glass. "Give me a boy, a grandson to bear the name!"

"Johnny may not have the name, but he's an Alston to his fingertips," said Maria. The dramatic edge to Maria's voice cut stingingly through the babble.

Theodosia felt giddy and sick. In their few weeks at The Oaks her health had already begun to decline and her attempts at being a good plantation mistress had been thwarted by house servants who resented her northern ways. She looked helplessly at Joseph, but her imploring glance was wasted.

Chapter Twenty-Three

Thomas brought the Alston chaise to the porch of the big house as he had done for three years now on the day after New Year's Day when the mistress took new clothing to Fairfield plantation. Looking around as he waited, he saw his mother approaching. A broad grin, showing gleaming white teeth, spread across his face. "Yuh git ticket?" he whispered hoarsely fearing for her safety.

She held it up to him. "I's be mighty hebby tuh look on yuh, ma chile," she greeted him. She emitted a short convulsive cough which took her breath away. The mile and a half walk from Fairfield plantation had been exhausting. Tom had been only seven when they took him from her to serve as a horseboy in the stables at Clifton.

Tom's eyes caught the work-worn hand, the shriveled skin over the thin aging arm resting for support on the carriage. "Yuh sho' look w'ary," said Tom.

"I git so wet las' spring ma skin sprouted watercresses."

"Why mekso yuh nebber wear de shoe?" Tom complained.

"I's keepin' de shoes fur de weddin'. De shoes, dem blonx tur me. Ma feet, dem blonx tur Maussa."

The doors of the big house swung open and liveried footmen appeared in smart Alston dark green broadcloth coats, vests trimmed in silver braid with red facings, and trousers of green plush. Tom and his mother stared nervously up the flight of stone steps leading to the porch. Suddenly Motte filled the doorway heavily cloaked, a veil over her face and large straw hat against the cruel sun. Tom's mother curtsied. "I'se come 'bout de weddin', Mistiss," she said timidly.

So many agonizing months had passed since Tom fell fatally in love with Olivia. Because communication with the slaves at Fairfield was frowned upon and he dared not be caught by the men who rode patrol, he had screwed up his courage to ask the "Maussa" for a ticket to attend his mother's birthday. The whole street of slave cabins were out beating the ground with sticks, shouting and singing. And there was Olivia, his ebony-black princess in a ring of dancers, their bare feet kicking up the dust, their hips swaying in frenzied movement. Tom caught her as she whirled out of the circle into the cheering crowd. They had wandered off into the starry night, the beginning of many tearful nights of parting because it was forbidden to marry a girl from another plantation. Tom, visiting without a ticket, risked detection by the dreaded men who rode patrol with fire in their bellies looking for runaways.

Motte was not deceived. She knew when any of the slaves were sick with love and she had guessed Tom's dilemma. William encouraged slave marriages. The birth of children in stable slave families contributed to a docile slave society. Several of their slaves married each year during the Christmas celebrations of good cheer, home bakings, and presents from the big house. Olivia was a sweet girl and an excellent seamstress, quite incapable of any mischief, Motte had urged William. He had been persuaded to make an exception. She looked graciously down at Tom's mother.

"The Master has given his permission," she said and smiled, touched by the slave woman's simple joy.

* * * * *

When Grandpa Joseph of The Oaks was alive he rarely visited his plantation Fairfield after he concluded the purchase. He left the running of it to Jackson, the overseer, a poor white from the pinelands who aspired to owning a plat of land of his own one day. The wages were good and the perquisites substantial—a house on the plantation, Negresses to cook and wash, and a houseboy in permanent attendance.

Jackson brought with him a young bride of Scots-Irish descent and between them they kept an iron hand on the field gangs, aided by whippings to subdue troublesome slaves. Overseer Jackson had no master to look over his shoulder the whole season through, from planting to harvesting. Grandpa Joseph and his family were always safely many miles away by rough road and row boats at their summer island retreat from the fever-ridden swamps. For three successive seasons, the brutality continued without Grandpa Joseph's knowledge, till disaster struck. Jackson's wife fell victim to swamp fever, and though he summoned a doctor immediately, who applied the usual remedies— bloodletting to reduce the fever followed by heavy doses of the bitter Peruvian bark—she died. Jackson took to the bottle, leaving the black driver in sole charge of the field gangs.

Whippings stopped, task allotments were lightened, the women helped themselves to rice for their cooking pots. Only one visit from Grandpa Joseph ever caused a flutter of conscience. The Fairfield rice brought to the flatboats for transport to the threshing floors did not compare with the good harvests at The Oaks, Grandpa Joseph complained. The black driver said nothing. "Damned bobolinks eating the young shoots," said Jackson. "I needs plenty Negroes to station in them plats, bird-scarin' and noise-raisin'.

Happen you might issue me with some shotguns, Mister, so they can kill 'um?"

"No shotguns," said Grandpa Joseph. "Children's holla'll scare'em yellow birds off."

That was the last they saw of Grandpa Joseph. Overseer Jackson went back to the bottle and the field gangs carried on at their own leisurely pace, till one day they heard over the grapevine that Grandpa Joseph was dead. The whole "street" mourned. In the row of slave cabins, old and young, fit or frail, waited in mortal terror, not knowing who had inherited them. Would the plantation be sold? Would families be split up? Would they be sold to different owners never to see each other again?

But William Alston, months after he inherited them, too upset by the shock of The Oaks going to his five-year-old son, simply threw out overseer Jackson whom he had caught blind drunk, and put in his own man with no whip as his emblem of authority.

• • • • •

Fairfield had been blessed with more than one overseer after Jackson, but none with today's task of issuing passes to an incredibly large number of slaves invited to attend a wedding at another plantation. Down the drive came Tom's mother leading a mile-long procession of singers and dancers, saucy women filing past in their Sunday best, jeering at dumbfounded men who rode patrol, defiantly waving their ticket. On every head was an offering for the feast—chicken, hams, wild turkey, and bakemeats.

William Alston of Clifton came onto the porch to propose the couple's health as soon as the Fairfield guests joined the Clifton Negroes in front of the big house. Negro spirituals filled the air as the house servants brought out hot wine and wedding cakes from the master's kitchens. Drummers and fiddlers started up the music. Dancers crowded the forecourt spilling over onto the piazza, while Motte's children played with the picaninnies and Algie, the only son of the family with a passion for rice culture—popular with the field gangs, often seen with the slaves casting nets for mullet and clamming, danced with a pretty slave girl who looked scared by his rascally, piercing eyes and the curious, stringy black hair combed over his forehead in a wavy fringe.

Piers came up behind Maria, leaning pensively over the piazza rail, watching hip-swinging, frenzied Negroes enjoying themselves. He had to shout to be heard. "Would you care to dance?" he said putting his hand on her arm.

"Good God!" she turned and said. "Have you actually torn yourself away from your books?"

"For you, I would tear myself away from life. I love you Maria."

"You should have gone north and sought another tutorship after the duel," said Maria. "We were mere children then."

"Leave this beautiful Carolina coast?" said Piers. "Here I am free!"

"What nonsense! We southerners are not free." Maria said looking at the crowd below. "George, Toby, Sunday, Hardacre, Moses, Daniel," she pointed them out. "Every Negro here is a chattel of father's. And we, too, are bonded, every planter family on Waccamaw."

"But you escaped," said Piers.

"You have no idea what it means. Being born into an elitist, fabulously wealthy family where slavery is established by law and the Negroes part of the whole fabric of society. You only have to listen to father."

"He does not buy and sell slaves at the Charleston slave mart," said Piers.

"He has no need. The slaves come with every plantation he purchases. And these weddings, how he encourages them. Tom and Olivia will have children, but from the day they are born they will be father's property to do with what he likes."

"You sound bitter, Maria."

"I'm just trying to explain to you that we, too, are bonded from birth by the system. Without the Negroes, we cannot survive."

"But you will break free again, butterfly. Go back to the stage."

"Butterfly?"

"That's what I always called you to myself."

Maria laughed spontaneously. "You silly boy! Well then, let's dance. Pretend we have no cares tonight." Her eyes shone bright, inviting romance.

Piers' pulse raced. He grabbed her tiny waist above the panniered skirt and whisked her across the lawns as though they had never been parted. This was the same blond Yankee who had fought so hard to keep his hands off the beautiful southern girl with the generous mouth curling at one corner. He remembered the devil in her eyes on the journey to New York, her tantalizing, shiny black hair he could not touch. Now they were coming together in an ecstasy of anticipation after the long different lives they had been living. Reaching the riverside spot they knew so well, Piers loosened Maria's hair letting it fall, as it used to, over her shoulders, forgetting the pangs of jealousy at the thought of Maria in John Nisbet's arms. His hands traveled gently as they laid together, he, holding back till she was aroused.

The sound was unmistakable—a galloping horse. Maria sprang to her feet. "Something's wrong. I left Johnny with Jacob."

Chapter Twenty-Four

For over thirty years black house slaves and white children in the big house had shared Mauma's love and understanding of the timidity of growing up and the emotions of adolescence. But lately she often repeated, "I sho' is w'ary Lawd. I'se ready fuh to go." The house slaves, seeing that Mauma's days were numbered, started showering her with little attentions for fear of the wrath of the ancestral spirits residing in the eternal baobab tree in their West African homeland where she, too, would soon be going. Although the master paraded them in church each Sunday on the benches reserved for slaves, and although they loudly praised Jesus's name, in the secret of their hearts they held firmly to the animistic beliefs of their forefathers carried down the generations by traditional storytellers. So Mauma's sudden appearance on the piazza gesticulating wildly before collapsing in a heap on the floor, after she had been tied to her rocking chair these past months, roused a prophetic cry of "de Lawd has set her sperrit free."

Many of the wedding guests had already wandered off to the street of slave cabins. Torches had been lit and their happy choruses rang through the night air, but a few stragglers still lingered in the yard below the big house as drummers and fiddlers packed up their instruments. One hefty young black took the initiative and rushed onto the piazza. Finding Mauma alive, he began gently raising her and barely caught her plaintive call above the din of wailing, "Please, Lawd, let 'um stay yere, let 'um lib, let 'um lib!"

But Mauma's prayers were not answered.

• • • • •

The angel of death hovered over the sickly rice swamps. The long gallop to fetch Dr. Murray presaged a victim of the dreaded cholera or yellow fever. Panic seized Maria as she raced back to the house assailed by a dreadful premonition. At the porch, she collided with Algie who was ashen-gray.

"Thank God you're here," he cried, his voice thick with emotion, but Maria had already leapt the spiral staircase.

"He's vomiting," said Motte sponging little Johnny's fevered forehead. "He's been calling for you," she said and stood aside. "Not black substance, not yellow fever, thank God. We don't know what happened."

Maria lifted little Johnny gently into her arms. "Mama is here, my darling. Oh, my darling, my baby," she said as she met his frightened eyes.

"Plat-eye come to take me," he sobbed.

"Hush, my darling. No one is going to take my little boy," Maria said as she pressed his feverish head to her breast. Suddenly she saw the hag holding a large calabash bowl. "What is that old woman doing here?" she screamed.

"She came with herbs, Maria, slave medicine," said Motte nervously as Maria chased the hag from the room. "The slaves think Johnny was bitten by a snake. My Jacob knows nothing."

"The hag's frightened Johnny with plat-eye!" Maria said as her eyes filled with hate. "Why isn't Dr. Murray here?" she cried, her mounting fear developing into hysteria. "Tell Mama darling. Did a snake bite you? When you're better darling we'll go and live in Philadelphia till Papa comes home. Remember all those things I told you about the theatre? And Fanny? My best friend? You're going to be so happy my precious."

◆ ◆ ◆ ◆ ◆

Little Johnny was buried in the private family burial ground at The Oaks plantation beside Grandpa Joseph's tomb. The words upon the headstone were Maria's own:

> "To the affectionately beloved memory of John
> Nisbet who departed this life on the 10 January 1802
> aged 3 years and 2 months. This stone is placed by his
> afflicted mother Maria Nisbet."

So stark, thought Joseph. So many things were going wrong since Maria's tragedy. Father was beaten at the February races, unheard of by the turfites. Motte gave birth to Frances Pinckney, who had hardly been christened before dying. There was no word from Nisbet. Maria was alone with her grief. Joseph had been to The Oaks Landing on the creek arranging a flatboat to row and pole Theodosia and himself on the morrow out of the creek into Waccamaw River and down the fifteen miles to Winyah Bay and the Alston Wharf at Georgetown. There, he hoped to find a schooner loading barrels of rice for shipment to Charleston, and a spare cabin.

What made him stop at the grave on his way back to The Oaks plantation house, he could not tell. His great-grandmother had first buried his great-grandfather in the private cemetery and called it "God's Acre". Its bricked in fence showed blood red in the setting sun. An evening breeze rustled the leaves of mourning cypresses. He was thinking, "I cannot reach her. Maria has become a stranger, my poor dearest sister." He had been angered by Theodosia's preoccupation with herself. Why did she have to refuse to go with the family to the summer house on Sullivan Island and have her baby quietly, without fuss, like any other respectable planter's wife? She had also refused his suggestion that the black midwife be fetched from Clifton. And now, she was imploring him to get rid of The Oaks mulatto overseer. Why, the fellow had been with the family for years, he told Theodosia. Then, she touched a raw nerve. "Calling himself Alston. Do you deny he is the offspring of a Negress brought to bed by someone in your family? He's insolent! Do you know what he said to me? 'De buckra hab scheme en de nigger hab trick, en ebery time de buckra hab scheme once de nigger trick twice.'" Her mimicry was perfect. Many Negroes adopt their master's name, he had flushed, but he could not dismiss her distress. She grew daily more sick and languid. He stepped across to his mother's grave. If Theodosia, too, should die in childbirth... He quickly banished the thought, but he left the cemetery a worried man.

• • • • •

After the tears, which would not be stemmed, came the guilt.

Dr. Murray, riven with pity for Maria, said, "You mustn't blame yourself. You must write your husband." The infant, Jacob, returning from shock had a recurring dream of a coiled snake. Motte took her frightened child to her own bed to be comforted in her loving arms. And Piers, sick at heart, could not help Maria. She did not want him. He brought only a painful memory.

• • • • •

Owls hooted and alligators barked just as they had over the moonlit marshes the night her beloved husband carried her across the threshold of her new home. Nothing had changed at Dean Hall Plantation since that delirious day of arrival, after their brief honeymoon with their lovechild stirring in her womb. Tragedy had brought Maria back to the place where she belonged, away from her father's house where there was no time in the bustle of activity for mourning the cruel loss of a child.

"Dear Fanny," she wrote, "I am broken. I pray God to bring him home..."

Chapter Twenty-Five

'Very early yesterday morning on July the eleventh of this one thousand eight hundred and fourth year of our Lord, right beneath the rocky heights of Weehauken in New Jersey, Alexander Hamilton and Aaron Burr faced one another ten paces apart. There was a double report the shots following in such rapid succession the seconds could not agree who fired first. Hamilton, clutching wildly, reeled and fell forward on his face.'

"Hey, Maria!" shrieked Fanny. "Read this! Joseph's father-in-law, our famous vice president, has shot Mr. Hamilton."

"Oh, God!" Maria said as she snatched the newspaper. Her eye traveled to a stop-press entry: 'Hamilton died at two o'clock this afternoon.' "I'm real sorry for Joseph. Theodosia will be shattered!"

"Her father will be tried for murder," said Fanny.

"Whites kill whites in duels at the drop of a hat," said Maria.

"Only ordinary people defending their personal honor," said Fanny.

"Politics! Politics! Politics! Joseph speaks of nothing else," Maria said beating the air with her fists.

"Aaron Burr has seen to that all right, Maria. Think of the damage now."

"I don't know what to do. Joseph and Theodosia are on holiday at the castle. They won't have heard. Don't you remember Hamilton in the auditorium of the Park Theatre, Fanny? Willy Dunlap saying 'D'yer think that smart aleck will recognize himself as Bland in my play?'"

"Burr also came to see *André* that night. I saw them both, and if only looks could kill. Everyone knows they've been rivals for years."

Maria turned over the page. "What a story!"

"Let's see," said Fanny peering over Maria's shoulder. Hamilton accused Burr of treachery and corruption, they read. Both men were orphaned in early childhood; both were precocious and entered college early; both enlisted in the army and fought under the same flag; both studied law and soon became eminent in its practice; both had good looks—Hamilton's eyes blue and deep-set, Burr's black and piercing; both were of distinguished address; both were leaders, but Hamilton was a natural orator and the greater lawyer. These two ambitious men were rivals at every point of contact. "You know what

Theodosia will say?" Fanny said as she drew back. " 'Well, that's one political enemy father will no longer have to worry about.' "

"You still love Joseph don't you?" said Maria. She had caught the malice in Fanny's throwaway line.

• • • • •

People began whispering that he had deserted her. More charitable neighbors put the blame on the escalation of the war with Napoleon's grand sweep across Europe calling all men to take up arms. She's no age, others said, only twenty-six. Most of our southern girls have just wed. She'll have many more children. Wonder how long she'll stay over at Dean Hall? She'll not be short. Rice prices are sky high. Those European armies have to be fed. There was so much gossip which did not reach Maria's ears.

Maria had gone into retreat. She was on the edge of silence, for she could not escape the familiar thud, thud, thudding of pestles in mortars on the flagstones each morning, house servants chattering in their native Gullah, singing at their work. She gave no orders and the slaves and servants simply absorbed her in the rhythm of their daily lives. They let her suffering and rage go unremarked like the passive river beyond the brown earth in its winter somnolence.

• • • • •

Sarah and John Ashe dropped in on their way to the races. Joseph brought news of the birth of their son. "Theodosia's calling him Aaron, which has upset father, who thinks he should be called after me," said Joseph. Algernon came to tell her that he and Mary of the double 'l' branch of the family were getting married as soon as she had discarded her widow's weeds. She could not recall Mary's first husband. Charlotte had come to stay a couple of nights. And always they asked if she had news. John had written he wanted a divorce, but she said nothing.

Then, one day she wandered along the slave street, and had come across old Humpy seated on a bench outside his cabin.

"I'se jes' waitin', Missis. I'ole an' w'ary." He rose slowly, bent and lame. His deeply wrinkled face opened up, and in his smile Maria saw a fierce dignity.

The street was quiet enough. A few children scampered about and were watched over by old women. In the distance blurred figures on the rice plats were completing their day's task. Suddenly, she wanted to talk, like one does to a stranger one may never see again. "Were you born here, Humpy?" She relaxed beside him on the bench, mindless of his reply. Instantly, he began his story, speaking the Gullah of the plantation Negroes, his excitement rising with each remembered time, and a strange glow in his eyes. Another life unfolded, which was a mirage of the same life. That boy of the forest, whose land is called Sierra Leone, meaning roar of a lion, unfolded his story. Maria's attention was at once engaged. In her vivid imagination he invoked the mystical lion mountain rising out of the sea covered in dark forest, the theatrical effects of fork lightning, the captive thunder roaring through the mountain peaks, the screams of victims of storm and crosscurrent disasters at the mouth of the Sierra Leone River. He spoke of his little fishing village on the snake-infested tropical Banana Island in the bay of Sierra Leone, and of its fertile rice swamps, bananas, limes, paw-paw fruits, and the sound of warning drums when slavers entered their waters.

She learned how by a curious twist of fate witchcraft was practiced upon their small community for the life of a child allegedly devoured by a leopard and the cruel punishment exacted by the king of the river. They must drink red water, the killer poison, or be sold to the slave traders. They chose the slaver ship as the lesser evil, but of the horrendous middle passage across the Atlantic, he could not speak. Better was death for those thrown to the sharks.

"If you had your freedom, would you go home to your Banana Island?" she said. Maria thought of plat-eye. "Paint 'um doors blue to keep out plat-eye." That's what Mauma had told her. Witchcraft had not been left behind in Africa. But Dr. Murray was quite firm, nothing could have saved Johnny. That old hag never gave him a drop of her medicine.

"I kin dream o' dat place," said Humpy, "but dat time pas'. S'pose yuh wan' tur go? Yuh hanker a't' de fooles' t'ing. Dis our lan'. We ax dem forest trees. We plant dem swamp," he said as he swept his hand slowly in an arc as far as the eye could see. "I wan' tur stay yere tuh de en'."

Maria fell silent. The old Negro's story had forever altered for her the dimensions of everyday things. Shortly after, she left Dean Hall Plantation. She went back on the stage accepting a small part in Nichol's new play, *Jefferson and Liberty*.

Chapter Twenty-Six

The beach house on Debordieu Island, a mile or so as the crow flies from The Oaks, had the nickname "The Castle" because of its large ugly structure raised from the ground by a huge impregnable fortress of heavy timber. But for Theodosia, this lonesome spot was a haven to which she and her adored infant son could retreat from the plantation life she loathed. Her spirits rose. Here she could wander over the sand dunes, free for a while from the demands of plantation mistress. Here she could watch great breakers lash the wild Atlantic shore. Here she could breathe the exhilarating sea air after the fetid swamps from which there was no letup.

When her father first met his grandson, little Aaron had called him Gampy and promptly extended the name to include himself to Theodosia's delight—big Aaron, little Aaron; big Gampy, little Gampy—the identities of her two passionate loves fused.

Rounding on Joseph when he delivered the news of the duel between her father and Hamilton, she said, "Everyone knows Hamilton nursed a bitter hatred of father."

"It is rumored your father has gone into hiding," Joseph fumbled his words nervously. "A great wave of popular feeling has followed the death of Hamilton. There is no place for your father here, Theodosia."

"Father has many friends in New York," Theodosia allayed Joseph's fears. "The charge against him is preposterous." But in her heart, she knew her father would find a way of reaching her. Worrying herself sick with waiting, she kept an anxious ear night and day for any stealthy footfall, a messenger perhaps, even her father himself.

* * * * *

Joseph invited them to call by, and they were gathered on the verandah of his Oaks plantation house sipping a lime punch when it happened.

The Alston branch of the family had left Brookgreen not an hour earlier, except for Maria, whose absence at the engagement party for Algernon and Mary had set tongues wagging. But then, competition between the Clifton Alstons and the Brookgreen Allstons, of the double 'l' branch, had been obsessive from the time of the first Beaufort landings.

Two of the sons went north to explore the Waccamaw forest and got into a scrape over a beautiful girl of Parisian elegance. The victor sealed his claim with the insertion of a second 'l' to the name. Their son, William, who had created the fabulous Brookgreen plantation out of the Waccamaw wilderness, adopted his mother's elegant style of living, inspiring the nickname "Gentleman" William. Had "Gentleman" William lived, things might have been very different for his second wife Rachel. Why, she continually asked herself, did he have to come home to die of fever? Why did she let him go to fight the patriot cause in the first place when he was already middle-aged? That he had returned a hero was no consolation. Instead, he had left her with a heavy burden bringing up his children by his first deceased wife as well as their two—Ann and Washington. What anxieties he was causing her now, her beloved Washington, going off to England, leaving his native Waccamaw to travel and paint. His portraits hung in galleries on both sides of the Atlantic. But Rachel sighed daily to have him home. She feared he was not looking after himself properly, living like a Bohemian among his friends. Lately, her thoughts had been elsewhere. Whatever would "Gentleman" William have said of his daughter, Mary, by his first wife bringing a single 'l' cousin into the family? He would have forbidden it after the two disastrous Alston marriages of Maria's and Joseph's. Yes, he would have forbidden the union between their two houses and if Mary had been her child she would have forbidden it also. But, Rachel complained, her stepdaughter was willful.

At Joseph's place, Algernon was being roughed up by his brothers. "Mary Allston is a real ogress of a plantation mistress, I'm told," said John Ashe.

"All the better for that," Colonel Alston intervened. "She'll not stand any nonsense from the house servants," he cast a disapproving look at Theodosia. "And she'll bear you many children, Algernon."

"But first cousins, Pa. What say you to that?" Joseph was annoyed at the jibe.

Colonel Alston chose to ignore the remark. In the attitude of a man about to address a public meeting, he said, "I am giving Rose Hill plantation to Algernon as a wedding present." As he spoke he turned proud, hawkish eyes on him. "I know how deeply your heart is in the culture of rice, my boy. You are my true son." He would have said more, but for the sudden interruption.

There was a scuffle outside and footmen tried unsuccessfully to prevent a visitor from entering. Perplexed, Joseph hurried forward to be met by Aaron Burr, his clothing travel stained, the broad grin on his face an insolent reminder of his irrepressible spirit. Instinctively, Joseph knew he had been tricked. Theodosia rushed past him to welcome her father. Joseph was utterly at a loss to know what to do. He looked toward his father whose very silence was nerve shattering. Motte was fanning herself agitatedly, and his litter sister, Charlotte, sat transfixed anticipating a storm. Sally choked upon a sweetmeat as John Ashe pushed her to one side.

In desperation, Joseph expostulated with Theodosia as she exclaimed, "Is the vice president of America to be treated like a hunted criminal?"

How Joseph resented the closeness between Theodosia and her father. However, he looked directly at his father. "I cannot refuse shelter to a member of my wife's family," he announced. His lips compressed, he took Theodosia firmly by the arm. "I order you to have your father taken to the guest chambers where he may refresh himself and await our pleasure. This is my house, and in my house I am master."

"Come father," Theodosia winced but yielded. "Let us go," she said and with her arm through his they departed together.

♦ ♦ ♦ ♦ ♦

As soon as the last Alston chaise had rattled off down the avenue of live oaks, the eerie Spanish gray moss that hung from their great boughs fluttering after them, Joseph gave vent to his rage, certain that Theodosia had plotted that Aaron should appear when all the family was gathered together.

But Aaron dismissed his outburst with a scornful, "Come on, my boy!"

Outfaced, Joseph began nervously to fondle his beard.

"You have the gift of oratory, you have studied law, I have given you introductions to men in the highest places of honor."

"Men who have turned against you!" Joseph commented sharply.

"Father has no fear of the howling mob." Theodosia intervened. "He is just keeping out of sight till passions subside."

Drawn reluctantly back into the web of his own ambition, Joseph appealed to Theodosia. "You don't want me to go back into politics." He had settled into a comfortable life as one of the wealthiest planters on the Neck. Most of all, he looked forward to his daily hour with his small son.

"I am in agreement with father," Theodosia astonished him.

He thought for a long moment and then said, "Very well, but on one condition."

"Yes?" Aaron frowned.

"That you make your way back to Washington without further neglect of your duties as vice president."

Aaron had not expected this condition. It was not that he was a coward. He had met greater hazards, but the bitterness against him for the death of an elder statesman was unparalleled. He was apprehensive, but he was also broke and he needed not only Joseph's approbation but also his immense resources as surety. He held out his hand to Joseph, "Very well. It's a bargain. Tomorrow I will travel openly to Washington in defiance of the charges leveled against me."

Chapter Twenty-Seven

They poured into Fanny's apartment to greet Maria like a long-lost friend. Never was there a happier sight. Tommy Wignell would have been thrilled. The whole of his amazing company, top actors from his Chestnut Street Theatre, the pride of Philadelphia, was exchanging warm, friendly, and witty stories. Farcical Jimmy Fennell, popular six-footer both on and off the stage, was relating, with hilarious panache, how he'd just lost a fortune speculating, of all things, in salt. Georgina Oldmixon was back on the stage in splendid voice after her long absence producing children. Ann Merry was shrieking "Maria darling!" and floating across the room under the jealous eyes of Mrs. Owen Morris whose bright star had been rudely eclipsed when Ann arrived from the English stage.

"Thomas spoke of your extraordinary power of moving an audience," Ann said as she smacked a kiss on Maria's cheek.

"I was sick with fright when he gave me that part in Willy Dunlap's *The Fatal Deception*" said Maria. Her eyes shone. Ann Merry who had been her idol had just been acclaimed the new Sarah Siddons for her Belvidera in *Venice Preserved* then showing at the Park Theatre in New York. "What made me curl up with nerves was seeing you there sitting through the dress rehearsal. It was a shambles."

Ann let out an infectious peal of laughter. "Thomas thought he had made a discovery in you, and then you flitted."

"I was expecting my husband to return from Europe."

"Just on a visit, she was," said Fanny. "Simply had to tread the boards! Well perhaps she won't go running off again this time."

"That's what I did, would you believe it?" said Ann, striking an attitude of lost cause. "Just fifteen, I was, when I first appeared on stage. It was our beloved Willy Dunlap who found me; he saw my début at Covent Garden. Silly me," she paused for effect. "I fell in love with Bobby Merry and retired from the stage to marry him. If Bobby hadn't lost all his money I would never have gone back on the stage, nor would I have accepted Tommy Wignell's offer to come over here to the Chestnut."

Bill Wood cocked his ear. He was a fanatical diarist. He listed all the plays of the season and penned details of the players, in performance and off-stage, with startling perspicacity. Right now, he was watching Mrs. Owen Morris's stricken face.

"My first appearance here was in 1796 as Juliet," Ann Merry continued unaware that she had ripped Mrs. Owen Morris's last rags of control. The wounded actress clawed her way to the door and rushed out.

Everyone waited.

"That was a remarkably fine exit scene," Warren broke the tension at last moving across to Ann. He and Bill Wood had become joint actor-managers after Tommy Wignell's untimely death, leaving Ann a widow for the second time. How he had wooed the gorgeous Ann. How difficult it had been to persuade her to marry him. He took her arm. "Now, now my beautiful adored leading lady..."

And the hubbub of the guests started up again.

"Ann's quite insensitive to other actresses' hunger for success," Fanny whispered to Maria. "I wonder what my dearling Bella, our Methuselah of the theatre, would have made of Ann?"

"Did they bury Bella under the timbers of the John Street?" Maria mused.

"They've never laid her ghost, that I do know."

Maria searched faces, drunk with drama, for a meaning to her own life. She had been in a state of collapse after John's cruel letter. One word, one gesture of kindness, and her self-control would be gone. John had written he wanted to marry his mistress, Rosina Byron! The name froze upon her lips.

◆ ◆ ◆ ◆ ◆

The November-December 1805 state session in South Carolina's new capital, Columbia, closed with Joseph taking the speaker's chair in a ceremony memorable for the versatility yet terseness of his address, the ring of literary command. His father, with rare pride in him, chose to celebrate the occasion with a grand banquet at Clifton, calling all his family together and inviting the entire plantocracy on Waccamaw.

It was a hard decision for Maria and Fanny. Maria could not let Joseph down, but Theodosia's child drove her to insane fits of jealousy and remorse. Fanny could not let Maria down when Maria begged her to join the party, but she raged at the thought of meeting Joseph's wife for whose beauty and wealth she had suffered defeat.

They arrived late. The house was swinging with merriment on Colonel Alston's famous wines, imported from France. Maria made an entrance, holding her head high as Homer announced Lady Nisbet. Fanny curtsied, dropping her eyes wishing the floor would open as she saw Joseph fight his way to greet his sister. Motte mistook her blushes for shyness and led her toward a pale aesthetic-looking young man who was staring after Joseph. "Piers," Motte called. "Let me introduce..."

Down along the streets of slave cabins the field hands lazily swatted river flies, chanted haunting spirituals to express their yearning for a faraway African homeland their generation had not set eyes on.

All at once the whole sky was alight and stretched red like a setting sun. "Gawd!" someone cried. "De night stan' lak de day. Sh'um yere de big house all aflame!" Suddenly they were being rounded up to rescue the mansion's priceless contents before it was completely gutted.

Colonel Alston took command with military efficiency and had the tables brought out from the burning building, the silverplate intact, the victuals hardly disturbed and the wine saved. "The party will go on," he raised his voice above the crackling timbers, the excitable babble of horrified guests, his imposing figure silhouetted against the bright night sky. Soon his beautiful home would be a heap of ashes yet not a bead of sweat moistened his brow though the heat from the fire was intense.

"When the night is finished we shall repair to my plantation at Fairfield." He turned to the field hands. "Take all the furnishings you can save to the overseer's house."

"However did it happen?" Maria's theatrical voice rose above the chattering crowd. She scanned the faces of frightened Negro house slaves lighted by the burning wreckage.

"My God! What a spectacle!" Joseph shouted.

Homer's smart livery was besmirched and torn. "Refill the glasses!" the Colonel commanded. "We have no need of tapers. All the heavens are ablaze for our enjoyment."

Maria caught the glint in her father's eye. "He's playing God," she thought, "taking all his bemused soot-covered admiring guests by storm. Tomorrow will be the day of reckoning. He is the perfect host, or just an actor!"

* * * * *

The consequences of the great fire completely overshadowed Theodosia's anxieties over her father, while Joseph's election as speaker had restored his self-confidence. Even though the legislature expected him to begin his speeches with that embarrassing stammer, they were prepared to wait patiently for the brilliant piece of oratory that he could be depended upon to deliver.

Aaron Burr's troubles were no longer news. Everyone knew that his political influence was broken and that he, encumbered by debt, had been forced to sell his Richmond Hill mansion. Only Theodosia knew that the revenue from the sale fell far short of his creditors' needs. She had not answered his last letter begging money from Joseph, reminding her that he was but forty-nine years of age and in his prime, that in New York he was to be disfranchised, and in New Jersey hanged, and that having substantial objections to both he was proposing to seek another country.

Chapter Twenty-Eight

The great fire also turned the tide of affairs for Maria and Fanny.

"She's beautiful. You can tell Joseph is devoted," said Fanny.

"You're too kind Fanny. Seeing Theodosia with her child leaves me desolate."

"I know. It doesn't ease your pain."

"I'm jealous Fanny. I hate her!"

"Why don't you go back to Philadelphia, Maria. Don't wait for me darling, don't miss getting a good part when the new season opens. It's too important."

"D'you think I would leave you Fanny?" said Maria. Flushed with emotion, Maria grasped Fanny's hand between hers.

Fanny's lungs were in a deplorable state. Dr. Murray had blamed the fire and had insisted she be taken to Georgetown for some clean air and rest. But, behind the footlights, Maria thought otherwise. Fanny's decline, she declared, was a consequence of overwork, poor lodgings, and the effect upon her nervous temperament of the stormy life of the theatre.

"I don't think I can face the behind-the-scenes embroilment," said Fanny.

"Of course you can't, Fanny dear. You have to get better. If we have another season like the last, then God help us! Oh God, it was savage! Our audiences won't stand another round of political farce melodramas. Willy Warren has got to give them some serious drama."

"Can Ann Merry play a variety of parts?" Fanny said wistfully yearning for a break from playing minor roles herself.

"Married to our actor-manager? She'll get them anyway. She's a tempestuous beauty!" A thought occurred to Maria in a flash of brilliance.

Georgetown's bustling commerce owed its prosperity to its favorable location at the confluence of the Sampit, Pee Dee, Waccamaw, and Santee Rivers flowing into Winyah Bay, which was navigable to shipping. Long before the English invaders, long before Grandpa Joseph's forebears pioneered this jungle sixty miles north of Charleston and settled along the banks of the great river Siouan tribals call Waccamaw, Siouan Indians used these waterways. But now it was the memory of Grandpa Joseph's rebel roll of Patriots that ran like a river through every Georgetown drawing room—Georgetown, the battleground of freedom from the English colonizers, home of Swamp Fox, hero of the War of Independence.

Maria was vehement, excited. "We have a captive audience. The town is full of professional people, middle-class entrepreneurs of English descent, French Huguenots—and no theatre!"

"Start a drama group? It's crazy Maria!" said Fanny.

"I need a challenge Fanny. We'll bombard that loquacious young partner of Joseph's. It's good they've opened a law office here. We'll invite Lyde Wilson to supper."

"Alone? Maria you're incorrigible!"

"We'll ask Jock Murray to come along. He's a bit of a dour Scot. He might throw cold water on the idea."

"But that fellow Wilson, he's obsequious. Ugh! Makes me go goosey all over," Fanny curled herself up into a ball.

"He's a lot of property in town. He's editor of the *Gazette*, and a prolific writer. Think of it, Fanny. He might find us a barn, and even write a play for us." Maria paused as she racked her brain. "I have it. We'll ask him to write a drama around the Marquis de Lafayette. He's a local hero, in case you don't know. He came all the way from France, landed secretly on North Island, and drew his sword to fight alongside our Patriots. He absolutely detested the English. Oh, how they're going to love it!" Maria's eyes shone as she visualized an ecstatic audience gripped by a drama recreated from their own history.

"Brilliant! But we need a cast," said Fanny disenchanted.

"Charleston's Dock Street Theatre has been turned into the Planters Hotel," said Maria, ignoring Fanny's pessimism. "We can canvass out of work actors and actresses."

"But the church, it's pretty reactionary and religious sects do seem to flourish down south. We may be hounded out of town. And what will your family say? You could be badly hurt, Maria," Fanny stayed doubtful.

"What can I lose more than I have already lost Fanny? If I could wish, I would wish for little Johnny back. At least they cannot take my title away."

◆ ◆ ◆ ◆ ◆

"I will not agree to it!" Maria flared up.

"He's still asking for a divorce?"

"Oh, if I could get my hands round the throat of that Italian hussy, Rosina Byron" Maria said as she tore the letter open in a rage. It was not what she expected and the rage left her. "It's from Alexander," she looked up surprised.

"John Nisbet's brother?" Fanny said curiously.

"You remember the story, Fanny. They were orphaned when their parents were shipwrecked returning from New York to Dean Hall. If they hadn't left the boys in New York..."

"Didn't their uncle send them to their grandmother in Scotland?"

"After the Revolution they came back to claim their property."

"Wasn't Dean Hall confiscated?"

"It was restored to them. But Alex went off taking half the Negroes and settled upcountry. He couldn't stand the unhealthy swamps."

"Is he asking for money?" Fanny inquired.

"He wants to bring his family to live at Dean Hall."

"D'you think he's got wind of John's mistress? Thinks he may not return? Has designs on the property?"

"The plantation belongs to John and myself. He has no claim upon it," said Maria.

"What are you going to do?"

"If I had wanted to be plantation mistress—but I don't," said Maria as she flung her arms round Fanny's neck, tears of emotion streaming down her cheeks. "I can't bear the house without John. To have Alexander taking care of the plantation, you can't imagine the relief."

◆ ◆ ◆ ◆ ◆

Maria bought a house on the corner of Screven Street. The courtly young Lyde Wilson arranged everything—the house, the barn on Front Street, the Negro carpenters. Persuading Joseph Alston to join him in opening a law office in Georgetown was a scoop he congratulated himself upon, to be allied with the man taking the speaker's chair in Columbia. Soon there was to be an election for intendant of the town of Georgetown.

He intended to place his name before the electors. He relied on Joseph's support, and always with an eye to the main chance, he looked beyond Joseph to the family.

Chapter Twenty-Nine

Rehearsals for the new play, specially written by Lyde Wilson for Maria, began inauspiciously.

"Where's Lafayette? It's hard to imagine you a nineteen-year-old," Maria looked critically at the actor, who was playing the part of Lafayette, lumbering onto the stage, awkwardly clutching his scabbard.

"I'm thirty-six," said the injured actor who had only played small parts before.

"Lafayette was tall, slim, and dark. A very rich, conceited, young French officer who landed on our coast in dead secrecy to fight in General Washington's Army," said Maria.

"If you want me to throw up the part..." the injured actor turned purple with rage.

"I don't think you're suited to it," Maria tried reason.

"What's to be done?" said Wilson.

"Find a French Huguenot, someone in the town with a sense of theatre," said Maria.

"Ma'am, the town will not stand you including Negroes in the cast," someone called out.

"It was a Negro who first spotted Lafayette's boat creeping in under cover of darkness. It's in the script," said Maria.

"I refuse to play the part of Sally, who remains loyal to King George III. I'm a Yankee. I won't be a treacherous Loyalist favoring the British occupying forces laying Georgetown to waste," Fanny objected.

"Please, please Fanny, don't be difficult. There's not a Yankee in the play. We're in South Carolina remember. All you have to do is flee. You're in grave danger, being chased by a captain in Swamp Fox's rebel army of Patriots. You're terrified of being raped and dispatched with a bayonet through your heart."

"No one's given me a copy of the play," a voice called from the prompt corner. "How does it end?"

"Triumphantly! Lafayette is seen at the trial of the spy, André, committing him to be hanged. Shades of Willy Dunlap," Maria turned with an aside to Fanny.

"We'll never find an actor to play André," said Fanny.

"He doesn't appear. The last scene is set in our town. The Marquis de Lafayette returns to the place where he first landed to celebrate victory in the War for American Independence. Georgetown adopts him as their national hero," Maria said striking an attitude of wild exaltation.

"It's a play for men," the offended actor said. "Suppose I could take the part of a British officer."

"Well, you're no Swamp Fox," someone rudely quipped.

"And for crowd scenes," said Maria.

"I'll put a piece in the *Gazette*," said Lyde Wilson.

* * * * *

Maria gave a party. The town had raised a cry against her. The church and public servants were difficult. The family was too grand to be loyal. Her leading actor's appearance as Lafayette had to go. There was no place for such ranting in the theatre. He blamed the crowded stage in the final scene, which damaged his performance. All the applause went to Fanny's terror of the rapist, her dramatic exit crashing head-on into the scene-shifters blocking the wings. Perceived as farce, the applause brought the house down while Fanny rushed to the dressing room with tears of rage at incompetent backstage staff working in cramped spaces. During the faltering last act, the audience started fidgeting and began to leave before the after-piece. They strolled over to the Convivial Club for a tankard to cure the spleen.

But Maria was incapable of stopping.

* * * * *

After the difficulties of *Lafayette*, Maria looked for inspiration elsewhere. She was dying to play the part of Portia and she turned to the diaries of Lewis Hallam, pioneer of the professional theatre in America before she was born. The great man left England for Williamsburg, Virginia with a company of ten actors, and on September 15, 1752, gave *The Merchant* of *Venice*.

Maria could identify with the attitudes of that day, the antagonism of religious groups, the treading of the stage a crime. Lewis Hallam, too, had used a converted warehouse, his last home, and finally taken his company to Philadelphia exhausted from vitriolic attacks by church and government at his daring to build a theatre in New York. She billed herself as Portia to Fanny's Nerissa in *The Merchant* of *Venice*. "It is going to be a theatrical sensation," wrote Lyde Wilson, who plastered playbills all along Georgetown's Front Street.

Maria, at twenty-nine, was a romantic grass widow. Everyone knew the scandal over her sister, Charlotte's, love affair. They thought themselves safe and were startled at the sound of footsteps. The black serving wench stifled a gasp of surprise, her hand covering her mouth. Missy Charlotte with the young tutor! They begged her not to tell! The young tutor pressed a coin into her hand. "I'se nebber tek bribe!" Being a slave girl, she had shunned the coin fearful of being found with it, but she did not keep her mouth shut. Maria regarded Piers as her special property and some instinct told her she must not loosen her grasp. Remarkably like her father, she did the unexpected.

Her father had precipitately sold out his entire stud after his famous stallion, Gallatin, was defeated at the February races. Lesser planters discussed the event as if it were a national crisis as they gathered in Georgetown's Convivial Club. Some said he was a bad loser; others said that it was an artful bit of showmanship intended to divert attention from his defeat. That stallion had not lost a race in the past nine years. It was rumored he had been viciously struck by the groom just before the race. Any other planter would have sold that Negro slave; "King Billy" sold his stud.

Maria's hauteur, the arrogance that was her charismatic charm, was a protest, a protection. She was despairingly in love with her husband, and as she put it to herself, he must soon tire of that Italian hussy. Nevertheless, there remained in her heart a tender spot for Piers. Charlotte's had been a cloistered childhood, watched over by her stepmother, and the young tutor had been her first love. Not daring to acknowledge their feelings publicly, their secret stolen moments revolved around nebulous plans to elope. A terrible row divided family loyalties. Piers offered his resignation. Charlotte shed hot tears of mortification.

Maria decided to adopt the big sister attitude, and said Charlotte must come and live with her, that she thought she would include her in her cast. After all, Lewis Hallam's was a family theatre, brothers and sisters included in the cast. But, she reckoned without her father.

"Have you not hurt me enough, Maria?" he fumed.

"Will you have her run away with a Yankee?"

"I am accepting his resignation," he raged. "How dare the impudent fellow abuse the trust I placed in him after the two of you ran off to New York." I showed extreme forbearance then, he thought back. He had accepted that Maria had acted with teenage wildness, so violently self-willed. But oh, how vulnerable was his little Charlotte, motherless from birth, the likeness of his dear departed first wife. A suitor would have to be found. No lady must be left on the shelf, and she had already reached her early twenties. But, he was obsessively fond of her and kept her guardian within his sights. He perished the thought of her ever leaving home.

"But, Piers is an excellent tutor, dear," pleaded Motte. "Think of our children. They are devoted to him. Where will we find another with his literary gifts?" For she saw it clearly, Maria would usher Charlotte into Georgetown society, and her little flirtation with the poet would soon be forgotten.

"I will cast Charlotte as Shylock's daughter," thought Maria, "and she will fall in love with the stage." But she still had to find a Shylock.

Chapter Thirty

Joseph rode the King's Highway from The Oaks to Georgetown, a worried man. In his breast pocket he carried the anonymous letter delivered to Theodosia. "Your father has been spotted in New Orleans and arrested."

He burst into the law office they shared, "I'm glad to find you here, Lyde."

"Why Joseph, it's good to see you." Lyde idly picked up a copy of the *Courier*. "There's a tirade against you, Joseph."

'Speaker Alston shocks Waccamaw planters,' the bold headline glared at Joseph.

"They're saying Theodosia is filling you with liberal ideas from the Northern states," Lyde went on. "Your inflammatory speeches calling for prohibition are making you dangerous enemies."

"Again and again the House passes prohibitions against the importation of slaves into the state but the Senate always rejects them," said Joseph.

"Prohibition, eh? But your own wealth depends on slave labor."

"Inherited, Lyde. My slaves were left me by Grandpa Joseph. I cannot shelve that responsibility, but importing slaves from other states, that's greed, nothing but greed. I didn't come here to talk ethics. Have you got the file on Aaron Burr?"

Lyde searched the pile on his desk awaiting litigation. "Here it is," he said opening it. "Burr left New York as Jefferson entered upon his second term, displaced by George Clinton as vice president. Burr then drifts a fugitive down the Ohio River and goes into hiding on Blennerhassett Island. Harman Blennerhassett is said to be fabulously wealthy, an Irish immigrant and a close friend of Burr's. Not much to go on," Lyde looked up.

"Cunning as a 'gator, with only his periscope awash, my father-in-law. He and Blennerhassett are to be tried for treason. Tried for providing the means for a private military expedition against the friendly Spanish provinces on the southwestern frontiers of our country."

"My God! They were after the Mexican gold mines."

"Coveting the wealth of the Incas. Blennerhassett's mansion has been ransacked and a cache of arms found. The locals set the whole place ablaze."

"So what's troubling you, Joseph?"

"I've received this letter from Blennerhassett. He quotes Aaron Burr as saying: 'I can at any time give security on the vast estates and other property of Joseph Alston, esquire, of South Carolina.'"

"He's trying to extort money from you?"

"Blennerhassett says he was duped by Aaron Burr into providing the finance for their military escapade and now he is being hounded by creditors. I have treated Blennerhassett's demands upon me with silent contempt. Now he is threatening to publish a book on the projects and intrigues of Aaron Burr, implicating myself and others, unless I send him $15,000."

"Ignore it, Alston."

"I can't, Lyde. Theodosia is beside herself. I adore my wife. I have to do something."

◆ ◆ ◆ ◆ ◆

Acting has to be in the blood. Maria discovered shy, pretty, blue-eyed Charlotte simply hadn't got it. Oh, how miserable Charlotte had been. She cried and cried when confronted with reality. The claustral family life on the plantation had lent wings to her fancy, fickle as love itself,

Piers went back to his native soil, and in truth, he felt a sudden nostalgia for the place where he was born. He left protesting his innocence of no more than kisses to a father opposed in every way to his darling daughter falling for a Yankee immigrant. He left after an anguished scene with Maria, the interminable years of her marital tragedy, the yoke of their bondage. "We will meet again. I am sure we will meet again dear, dear butterfly."

And now, with so much to see and so much to do, Charlotte was secretly relieved that nothing could ever come of it, no entanglements.

◆ ◆ ◆ ◆ ◆

Joseph and Lyde came to dinner. It was always what Maria wanted, Joseph without Theodosia. It was not Theodosia's fault that she was convulsed with hatred for her. It was linked to the memory of her own lost happiness. But, she had forgotten Fanny. As soon as Joseph entered Maria read in Fanny's face the turbulence of her heart. She searched in vain for some conspiratorial response, but there was none. "How easily men erase the past," she thought. She said, with cutting edge, "What brings you to Georgetown, Joseph?"

"Another drama in the making Maria. Will you commission me to write a play?" Lyde intervened with calculated indifference.

"Shut up, Lyde. It's true. Theo's father has been at it again. He has raised a private army of malcontents and has been arrested on a charge of treason," said Joseph.

"And Theodosia wants to go to him," said Fanny. It was so predictable. Joseph was staring over her head now into nothing. He looked haggard, unhappy.

"I cannot let her go," he said at last. "She's in very poor health."

Charlotte twisted a handkerchief nervously round her fingers. Any talk of Theodosia always embarrassed her. Intuitively, she knew the whole family disliked Theodosia, but she had never moved forward from that first schoolgirl worship of her beautiful new sister-in-law. She wanted to say something nice, but the moment passed before she could form the words, for Maria had abruptly turned the conversation.

"We've got to call in a star to play Shylock!" said Maria.

"Oh my God, Maria. Don't you know the theatre is dead?" said Joseph.

"Just because those pious Charlestonians have closed Dock Street? What do you know of those out-of-work actors? Well, I'll tell you, they've formed a touring company." Maria was irrepressible.

"Well if they start traveling north they'll be right up against the Puritans!"

"The trail stops here, Joseph. I want them right now for *The Merchant Of Venice*," said Maria.

"Another ghastly production? Amateurs strutting about the stage?"

"You're insufferable Joseph. 'Fraid you'll find yourself a barely concealed character ridiculed on the stage? Politics! It's all a game for little boys," Maria said keeping up the banter.

"Who was it said 'I can at any time give security on the vast estates of Joseph Alston?'" Lyde mimicked with a wicked smile.

"Is that a proposition?" Maria seized upon it.

• • • • •

Joseph hurried home with nothing settled. For several months he had worried over Theodosia's declining health as she visibly languished under the strain of waiting for news of her father. "I beg you not to undertake the journey," Joseph urged. How he resented their devotion. But she was clinging to him, imploring him, and he could not bear her suffering. "Then I insist you drive in our own cabriolet. You are not well enough to use public transport."

Her face showing her gratitude, she said "Gampy will accompany me."

Joseph's mood changed. "It is no place for our son to be visiting."

"But father will be heartbroken!"

"No, Theo! It is for you to decide whether your father is worth the sacrifice of being separated from Gampy."

Theodosia bowed before his opposition. "You will see he has his lessons regularly?"

"Naturally, my dear."

* * * * *

The prosecution of Burr and Blennerhassett was not pressed and following his release from custody, Aaron Burr decided upon a self-imposed exile in Europe. "It is the only course open to me," he consoled Theodosia, "until all the fuss has died down."

Joseph had arrived to bring Theodosia home and Aaron turned to him. "It will be difficult to find a skipper," he said pointedly.

Joseph was prepared to pay a high price to see his father-in-law out of the country. "There is a British packet, the *Clarissa*, leaving shortly I hear. I will buy you a passage."

"To England?" Aaron said doubtfully.

"You have no choice," Joseph pressed. "You will, of course, have to change your name."

All the color drained from Theodosia's face but Aaron had recovered his spirits. "I shall choose the name Mr. Edwards."

"And I will stay with you until you are aboard," Theodosia threw herself passionately into his arms.

"It may take several days," Joseph remonstrated. "I can't be away that long." It was as he expected. But he gave no indication of his fears, that Theodosia might suddenly decide to embark with her father never to return.

Chapter Thirty-One

"Ann Merry dead! I can't believe it," cried Maria.

"Willy Warren is devastated!" Fanny began reading from Jimmy Fennell's letter. " 'Our supreme leading actress has died in childbirth and at only forty. The lights have gone out on the American stage.' " Fanny looked up, her face ashen. "There's to be a memorial service at the Chestnut. No date has been fixed."

"Ann would like that," said Maria.

"She was equally successful on the New York stage," added Fanny.

"But the Chestnut was home to her, built like the Theatre Royal, Bath in England, where she was first discovered. What a tragedy. She would have hated dying. Fought like a tiger," said Maria, but her thoughts were already dashing ahead—Ann Merry's blazing star so unexpectedly extinguished. "Fanny, darling," she fell into her coercive southern drawl, "don't you feel Georgetown's parochial after all?"

"I'm not sure what you're saying?" replied Fanny.

"Our being extravagantly billed as stars, Lyde's amazing talent for adding glamour to my Portia and your Nerissa to attract audiences, disguising we have a weak supporting actor for the loathsome Shylock, and clueless locals in minor parts—we must do something, Fanny," Maria challenged.

"Do?"

"Test ourselves. Confront wider audiences. Tour!"

Fanny's face lighted. "I'm homesick for Philadelphia."

"What shall we do about Charlotte?" Maria said. Maria was suddenly thrown into a quandary. "The dear sweet girl has delicate health."

"She's been happy here in Georgetown," said Fanny, "but I can't see her surviving the rough and tumble of hostelries."

Maria drew a visiting card from her purse. At the center of the thin white piece of pasteboard the name Lady Nisbet stood in bold copperplate characters. The sight of it had an emotional effect upon her. It wrenched her back ten years when to be an actress was all she dreamed of, until she fell blindly into love.

"You've got to forget that man," Joseph said repeatedly. "Don't you understand Maria? He's left you."

Below her own name, on the thin white piece of pasteboard, Charlotte's appeared—Miss Charlotte Alston. Maria knew that, once back at Fairfield, poor unmarried Charlotte's name would appear below Motte's name and Motte's chaperoning would be entirely at Papa's discretion. He would arrange a suitable union with one of the leading planter families on Waccamaw Neck.

* * * * *

"All the leading roles are for men," Maria complained.

"What about making a comeback with Mrs. Rowson's, *The Female Patriot*? It hasn't been performed for a decade." Maria was talking to a handsome man with graying whiskers, the one-time manager of Dock Street Theatre, who actually discovered her when she was at finishing school. On chancing to pass through Georgetown, he heard of Maria's attempts to form an acting company, and thinking she must be mad, got himself invited to a party celebrating their imminent departure on tour. "Darling girl, you are more beautiful than ever," he said and they had embraced with tears of inexpressible joy rolling down Maria's cheeks.

"But, don't you think we'll do better putting on a Dunlap play? He's all the rage. They say he writes a play a week."

"Farce melodrama caricaturing anybody and everybody, very sensational. Likely he'll write a stinging play on the intrigues of Aaron Burr next. But poor Dunlap, his management of the Park was a disaster. Two epidemics of yellow fever hitting the theatre. Quarrelsome actors and actresses throwing tantrums. He simply could not cope."

"Is the theatre closed?" asked Maria.

"Luckily, the New Yorker, Abthorpe Cooper has leased it." Maria's idol of her schooldays cast a critical eye around. "The Smugglers Players you call yourselves."

"Georgetown's middle-class patrons scoff," Maria grimaced. "Pretentious title they say for a building with only a platform at one end and a meager array of smoking candles for light."

"S'ppose you're financially secure?"

"Far from it. We've the editor of our local gazette drumming up interest." Maria scanned the barn. "Anyone seen Lyde? I must introduce you."

Nobody answered, for with sudden recognition, several of the company were making a dramatic charge to fête the man they had worked with before Charleston turned Dock Street Theatre into The Planters Hotel. Leaving him to their excitable welcome, Maria went in search of Lyde, and found him out on the promenade at the waterfront ablaze with the golden light of the sun dipping behind tall cypresses across the bay. What she saw caught her breath and she swiftly left. Lyde turned, fancying he heard footsteps, and saw only a flash of ballgown. He could not identify the intruder.

◆ ◆ ◆ ◆ ◆

A week had passed since Lyde found the courage to hand Charlotte the letter. At first she mistook it for a treatise for it covered more than twenty close-written pages delicately perfumed and tied with blue ribbon. She did not even think seriously that she was obliged to respond.   It began with a dissertation upon his intentions following his election as intendant. He would spare no effort to curb those hotheads who recklessly rode their carriages along the town's dirt roads churning up clouds of dust. He would allow no person driving a cart, dray, wagon, chair, chaise, gig, curricle, sulky, or other carriage to drive the same, faster than a trot.   No person would ride on horseback faster than a moderate canter under penalty of a fine. And, he continued, the whole town was enraged at the behavior of those young hooligans from the plantations. He promised to put an end to it if he were elected.

Page after page, Charlotte struggled through in a bemused sort of way. She was well used to his wordy editorials and so did not at once comprehend, when he abandoned his political rhetoric to speak of love's torment.   Joseph's best friend, who was to her no more than like a brother, had all at once become a desperate suitor. "He was not the kind of man I would choose," she had once laughingly said. But the letter was so explicit there was no way to avoid it. He had awakened in her phantoms of love, and it frightened her.

"You have not answered my letter!" Lyde said.

There was nothing gentle in Lyde's voice and Charlotte's heart missed a beat. Nervously she kept her eyes staring across the bay as he came up behind her. Now she could feel his hot breath down her neck. She felt physically weak, spiritually bereft. Without knowing why, she said uneasily, "Are you asking us to be lovers?"

He put his hands on her shoulders, swung her round and kissed her full on the mouth. "I am asking you to be my wife!"

◆ ◆ ◆ ◆ ◆

Charlotte had one of her feverish chills. Jock Murray sat talking to Maria in the parlor after attending to her. "The fellow's got boundless energy. He'll wear her out," said Murray.

Maria saw in her mind's eye the sun-drenched wavy hair, seductive curl over the forehead, dancing eyes, habit of half-smiling under high cheekbones. "But, he has irresistible charm when he wants to use it."

Jock rested his hand on his chin in thought. "Charlotte was upset when I told her her health would not stand touring. This is so sudden. Is Lyde in love with her?"

"With the family, Jock, though his proposal has come as a bit of a shock. Still he'll make a good husband, and God knows I wouldn't have her tied for life as a plantation mistress with constant pregnancies producing heirs hemmed in by rice fields and sullen Negro servants," said Maria.

"She has grown up amongst them. She speaks their Gullah as well as any."

"Ah! Dear, dear Mauma. I wish she were alive. We learned it from her, but how Charlotte has blossomed since she came to Georgetown."

"She is a lovely, unaffected girl, a real peach. Lyde is lucky."

"He's ambitious, our aspiring Georgetown lawyer and writer. Charlotte'll be expected to entertain every night of the week."

"I hear he's bringing out a book on dueling, all that waste of young life. Pistols drawn at the drop of a hat. What does Charlotte herself feel?" Jock asked.

"Panic-stricken! I advised her to tell him yes, even if she is dying of fear because she will be sorry for the rest of her life if she says no."

"And has she?"

"Poor Charlotte is so confused. Lyde has set a date for formalizing the engagement. But Charlotte is no rebel. It will be Pa who decides who she will marry and Lyde has yet to face him."

Chapter Thirty-Two

Theodosia returned, improved in health from a New York resort, only to weaken again in the treacherous lowcountry climate. The swampy rice fields behind The Oaks poisoned the air as they steamed under the early morning sun and her frustration worsened as the months went by.

Joseph, beside himself with worry, had a new summer home built at Greenville in the more salubrious upcountry. He urged her to stay longer than usual during the high season in Charleston. All Theodosia wanted was to be at the beach house on Debordieu Island and to wander among the sand dunes by the roaring Atlantic Ocean with her own thoughts for company. Her father had written begging her to voyage to England to consult with the most celebrated physicians in London. Joseph, knowing she would never return, was delighted to learn that Aaron's fortunes had taken a turn for the worse. Served with a warrant, he had been told at the Alien Office that his presence in Britain was embarrassing to His Majesty's government. But where was he now? Theodosia fell into another terrible depression.

If she would only help him in his tough campaign for the state governorship. But all she wanted was to have Gampy with her at The Castle. Here she undertook to teach him herself. Gampy's aunts at Fairfield, Hagley and Rose Hill plantations expressed concern at the child's frailty but Theodosia always answered that he had plenty of fresh air at Debordieu.

◆ ◆ ◆ ◆ ◆

The marriage of Charlotte Alston to John Lyde Wilson took place on old year's night at Fairfield in the presence of an exclaiming, gesticulating throng of adults and excitable children.

Maria amused herself at the element of the theatrical in her father. There was no sign of his early disappointment at Charlotte's engagement to a man with no history of rice culture in his veins. Accompanied by grandiose gestures, he declared his new son-in-law to be a man of many attributes with a promising future. He went on to speak of her dowry, an elegantly furnished clapboard townhouse in Georgetown's most select quarter, overlooking spacious, well-stocked flower gardens. He confirmed his confidence in Lyde. "He will make my sweetest, most dearly loved daughter by my poor lamented first wife, happy," he said dramatically wiping the moisture from his eyes. Lyde responded with a courtly bow before the assembled company.

"Speech, speech!" they cried. And with so many of the clan gathered together—the Brookgreen Allston cousins of the double "l" branch, Sarah and John Ashe with their two infants, Algie looking prosperous with his cousin-wife and a brood of children, Rebecca, Motte's eldest, already seventeen, débutante of the year, and Motte's fine teenage sons Thomas Pinckney, Charles, and Jacob, Joseph with Theodosia and her adored Aaron at her side—it was inevitable that the conversation should turn to politics.

"I have purchased ten thousand acres of untamed forest at Bull's Creek," said Colonel Alston. There was a stir of amazement.

"But it is uninhabited way up the Waccamaw," Joseph exclaimed. "Where will you get the Negroes to clear those wild acres?"

"Negroes by the thousands are being driven into the state from Maryland and Virginia," Algie answered quickly.

Ignoring his brother, Joseph continued. "You are all aware of my views on prohibition."

"But Algie is right," his father supported, "with the expansion in the upcountry of cotton."

"Many lowcountry politicians are apprehensive at the influx. The entry of Negroes from other states is both unjust and demonstrably injurious to our own!" Joseph flushed angrily.

John Ashe, remembering a scary holiday sleeping rough beneath a forest canopy, said, "Vicious vines, impenetrable twenty-foot high bamboos at Bull Creek."

"Fine fishing grounds," said Thomas Pinckney enthusing.

Algie who had modeled his plantation, Rose Hill, on Fairfield vigorously nodded his approval of the purchase.

Presiding over his offspring like some tribal chief, William Alston felt a glow of satisfaction. Long life and good health had enabled him, at nearly sixty, to retain his authority as absolute ruler over his vast domains, largest of all the slaveholders on Waccamaw and with sons guaranteed to succeed him in the culture of the golden grain. "Truly I am King of the Neck," his thoughts ran.

"Oh do let's stop talking rice for once!" Charlotte suddenly screamed pressing her hands over her ears. It was after this startled interruption that Maria saw her ten-year-old nephew Aaron break from his mother and come purposefully toward her.

◆ ◆ ◆ ◆ ◆

The boy stood nervously, his eyes fixed upon his aunt's bodice fascinated by the shimmering Eastern silk which changed color like a chameleon with the rise and fall of her chest. It was not nervousness that caused Maria's agitation. The boy was so blond, but his eyes were brooding dark beneath decided arched eyebrows, the nose Roman, the mouth finely chiseled like his mother's, a beautiful child but sickly-looking, Maria observed. "Nothing about him is like my Johnny," she was thinking. Johnny was so full of life. She had never ceased to harbor a seething jealousy of Theodosia and her child. Yet it was she alone the boy sought with fatal attraction on the rare occasion of a family get-together.

"May I sit with you, Aunt Maria?" he said in a plaintive voice.

"Why can I feel no affection for him?" Maria thought as she invited the boy to draw up a chair.

Aaron, as a ten-year-old, had a sort of hero-worship for his aunt. Maria walked beglamoured. He sought out every piece of news of her stage appearances. She was a star. Some day he would see her in performance. He said, "Papa wants me to go to school in England and when I come home I shall go on the stage. I shall travel and tour like you, Aunt Maria."

This brought a smile upon Maria's face. "You don't want to go on the stage, Gampy," she used his nickname for the first time in years.

"Mama is teaching me Greek and Latin and I play at acting characters from my Shakespeare."

"You will go to Oxford, Gampy. That's what your father wants, like the Pinckney brothers, two of your great Grandpa Joseph's Patriot rebels while they were still students in a foreign land."

"But I will not be a planter when I'm grown up. Do you know what some English soldiers did when we beat them in the Revolution? They stole thousands of Negroes as they retreated, promising them freedom, then sold them back into slavery in the West Indies. Papa's library is full of exciting stories about the Revolution."

"But what have they to do with your not wanting to be a planter like your father?" Maria asked.

Aaron passed over the question. Instead he said, "I want to be an actor-manager. I want to be like you."

Maria had a fearful vision of poor, damp, theatrical lodgings, the depredations of struggling actors that only the Herculean survive as she returned the boy's passionate gaze. But she said nothing.

"I think you are beautiful, Aunt Maria."

"You flatter me, Gampy. It's very sweet of you." And she bent down and kissed him lightly on the cheek.

Chapter Thirty-Three

When Theodosia received news that her father was at last on his way back to New York Joseph was in the throes of the fiercest campaign for state governor. Theodosia was beside herself with joy. Joseph was relieved to see her spirits rise and her health improve, despite his own embarrassment with Carolina rice planters in crisis, just as he was fighting for the seat of the highest honor of the state.

The boom in the price of rice had long been sustained by Napoleon's need to feed thousands of soldiers defending his huge land power across Europe, but the Carolinas on the other side of the Atlantic were now caught in the menacing jaws of England's massive sea power after Nelson's great victory at Trafalgar. Napoleon, in retaliation, was determined to starve out island Britons and had ordered that no neutral country or French ally was to trade with those intransigent peoples. Britain had promptly replied by issuing orders in council subjecting all Napoleonic Europe to blockade.

Crying, "Neutral flags make neutral goods", the rice princes had been making desperate attempts to break the blockade and enter European ports, but island Britain, ignoring the pleas of her once colonial territory, promptly gave her sea captains the right of search under the orders in council. With piratical audacity, these coarse sea captains were now mischievously harassing grain-filled frigates innocently leaving Charleston on their way up their own coastline with supplies for New England's fast-growing industrial heartland in the north. Daily, more and more rice plantations and Negro slaves were being put up for sale as markets vanished and planters were burdened by debt.

In the distant, magical Philadelphia theatre world, Joseph's troubled campaign for state governor in Carolina's deep south had no ear. It was Willy Warren's decision to revive *Venice Preserved,* his macabre desire to recapture the spirit of his beloved wife, astonishing actors and actresses alike offering the classic lead role to Maria Nisbet, that was the talk of the town. How could anyone follow Ann Merry's brilliant success? Maria had not the stature. Willy was out of his mind. Even Ann's obituary gave special mention to her beautiful tragic Belvidera, calling her early death a great blow to the American stage.

• • • • •

"It's mighty disappointing we won't be with you on your first night," wrote Charlotte. "Lyde is terribly pressed writing speeches for Joseph when he is not replying to vitriolic letters sent to the press. My husband is ad nauseam a duelist in words as you know too well, honey. Jock Murray will carry our luck card."

Maria agonized over the long arm of Sarah Siddons on the other side of the Atlantic. Ann Merry could not tear her Belvidera to shreds in caustic criticism, but Sarah Siddons was very much alive on the London stage!

"It's rumored Siddons is rehearsing for a farewell appearance as Lady Macbeth," said Fanny.

"Doubt she'll ever quit the stage. It was in the part of Belvidera that she rose to fame very early in her career. They say she never performed better." From among greasy substances and powder make-ups in her tiny cluttered dressing room Maria produced a fistful of criticisms. "I borrowed these from Willy Warren. Ann studied Siddons closely. She always wanted to be a tragedienne like Siddons. Listen to this acclaim of Siddons' power, 'Who shall make tragedy stand once more with its feet upon the earth and its head above the stars weeping tears and blood?'"

"I would be sick with joy if anyone wrote that of me," said Fanny. "But Belvidera, what a gift of a part!"

"One critic writes of the play," Maria went on, "that 'It gains strength and expressiveness as it proceeds. Eventually, we are almost convinced that in following the fate of Jaffeir, Pierre, and Belvidera, we are in the presence of classic drama of Racinian greatness.'" Maria picked up her script. "If only Thomas Otway hadn't written it in blank verse!"

Fanny took over the bundle of old press releases. "Here's one critic who calls the play 'a somewhat overwrought tragedy, a plot to overthrow the rulers of Venice with some of the attempts at Shakespearean grandeur of utterance occasionally raising a smile.'" She sighed a sigh of infinite envy. "Maria, you too, will be tragedy personified, a flame of passion!"

"I couldn't do better than have Willy Warren as Pierre. So extraordinary that he played in support of Siddons in those romantic early days when Siddons was touring the English provinces. That's where Tommy Wignell found him and persuaded him to join his troupe setting sail for Philadelphia."

"Yes, I'd forgotten the connection."

"Fanny, I'm really frightened! I wish you were in the play. It's marvelous acting with you. You're so wonderfully generous on the stage."

"Maria, I've got to tell you, when we've finished touring, I'll be quitting the Smugglers. I can't take another dose of that awful climate in the deep South."

For once Maria did not strike a dramatic attitude. She had lost a private battle for revival of the theatre in Charleston. Fanny's enthusiasm for building a theatre in Georgetown had been an inspiration. She thought of their first acting parts together in New York—Mrs. Racket and her sister Caroline in *The Father,* actor-manager Johnny Hodgkinson's high drama on and off the stage, their terrible disappointment when he withdrew the play over a row with Wignell's rival troupe. Oh, the passions, the loves, the hates, and the sheer exhilaration of being part of the John Street and the Park. Glorious times, she and Fanny had lived through, and the whole future still before them.

"Oh please, Fanny, we can't do without you," Maria implored when suddenly she was gripped by a chilling fear. Fanny stood there thin and pale, looking as if a puff of wind would carry her off. Lottie Hodgkinson died of consumption, the ugly thought flashed across Maria's mind. She fell silent again.

"Father is sick," said Fanny. "I have been sending money but he's pleading with me to return to New York. He says there's work. More and more theatres are springing up. They are even talking about building a theatre at the Bowery alongside the Bull's Head tavern."

"That brings back memories! Joseph had an apartment on the Bowery. He was great when Piers and I landed on him after I ran away from home." Maria looked wistful. She was thinking, with Fanny a thousand miles away in thriving New York, and remote swampy Georgetown showing little enthusiasm for the theatre, she would feel terribly cut off and desolate!

• • • • •

At The Castle on Debordieu, Theodosia was making elaborate arrangements for the arrival of her father. He had written her from Sweden in buoyant spirits praising the Swedes for their admirable system of jurisprudence and congratulating them upon their good roads, going on to say they had treated him as a distinguished guest, even receiving him at court and taking him to the reputed tomb of Hamlet.

"How I pine for you and for my little grandson," he wrote. "I have gifts for you my darling Theodosia, fine fabrics, stone settings, books, and a collection of beautiful medals for Gampy. I have repeatedly applied for a passport to reenter young America but always my application has been turned down. Now, I am risking everything to come home. I have changed my name to Adolphus Arnot and have persuaded the captain of the *Aurora,* shortly sailing for Boston, to take me on board."

Joseph rode his favorite bay along the sand dunes, grateful for the ocean breeze. Spending the night at The Oaks upon returning from a grueling week in the state capital, he had slept badly under a net in the intolerable June heat and humidity. Along his way to join Theodosia and Gampy at Debordieu, he passed rows of his own field hands singing a ditty in time with the plod of their hand hoes as they removed trash from the young rice shoots. The long water flooding had been drained off and dry cultivation was at its height before the final flooding. He remarked at the health of his rice plats, envied the slave women bent over their hoes sweeping across his fields like gentle waves with no apparent stress, as he perspired profusely, soaking his shirt, filling his eyes with salty drops off his brow.

Tired and irritable, Joseph arrived in a scolding mood. Theodosia should have taken his advice and gone with the rest of the family to the summer house on salubrious Sullivan Island. Receiving no sympathy from Theodosia, he turned his mind to asking about Gampy after missing his son who always ran to meet him excited at his father's homecoming, but no one had seen Gampy in the last hour. Perplexed, Joseph sent out a search party taking to the sand dunes himself where the boy loved to roam. Suddenly he saw a Negro bend down behind a tuft of sea grass. Rushing forward he pushed the slave aside and picked up his whimpering child.

"What is it, Gampy?" he said anxiously, thinking only minutes earlier he had passed so close to where the boy lay without seeing him.

"My head!" said Gampy as he put his hand up.

A cold hand of terror clutched Joseph's heart as he carried the boy back to the house. "He must be put straight to bed and given the bitter bark," he called Theodosia.

"But Gampy hates the medicine," Theodosia argued. "It's only a chill from the changeable sea breezes," she said putting her hand to Gampy's forehead. But seeing the fear in Joseph's eyes she softened. "He'll be fine in the morning," she said wrapping a shawl round Gampy. "You must not go running outside darling till your cold is better."

◆ ◆ ◆ ◆ ◆

By morning Gampy was much worse, with a high fever that made him delirious. Joseph sent a rider galloping for a doctor and forced Gampy to swallow the bitter bark. Throughout the day and into the next night the two terrified parents stayed by his bedside praying for a miracle when suddenly Gampy raised himself on his pillow.

"Mama!" he cried. And again, "Mama!" Then he fell back exhausted. "Mama is here, my precious, my darling," Theodosia said as she smothered him with kisses taking him into her arms. In a petrifying silence, broken only by Joseph's sobs, Theodosia caressed her beloved child now beyond all help and comfort.

◆ ◆ ◆ ◆ ◆

Gampy was laid to rest beside his little cousin, John Nisbet, in "God's Acre", the Alston burial ground at The Oaks. There was no time to gather the family together with everyone away at their holiday retreat escaping the sickly season. In the intense heat, burial could not be delayed.

Theodosia haunted The Castle continuing strangely mute and tearless. Joseph thought her still numb from shock. At last, he could bear it no longer. He sat down and penned the most painful words of his whole life.

> "One dreadful blow has destroyed us. That boy who was to have transmitted down the mingled blood of Theodosia and myself, that boy at once our happiness and our pride, is taken from us—is dead!"

Chapter Thirty-Four

Jock Murray was the first to congratulate Maria in a rare show of emotion. "Darling you were magnificent!" said this dour son of a Scottish immigrant who burst unceremoniously into her dressing room. She threw back her head and her shining eyes were full of laughter, radiantly drunk with the elixir of a personal triumph, still in her ears the long silence of suspended animation as the curtain fell and then thunderous applause.

"Oh, what an ovation!" Jimmy Fennell said, putting his head round the door. "Supper at the tavern in ten minutes folks," he called along the passage.

Mrs. Owen Morris pushed through. "I have to say it. You gave a strong performance m'dear. Your Belvidera was a startling innovation. It lifted the whole play for me. Whatever happened to Willy's Pierre? One moment I really thought he'd get the brickbats."

Maria wiped the laughter from her face. Willy Warren had acted mechanically with a dead hand on the character. "He didn't seem to be in the part tonight," she said. "I think it got me overacting once or twice."

"Well, no one can say your Belvidera was an attempt to imitate Ann."

"P'rhaps that's what Willy wanted, an image of his beloved Ann in my Belvidera."

"So, he started drowning in his own sorrows."

Maria flung off her costume. "Was it a mistake? It wasn't the memorial he expected. God! I'm hungry. I could eat a horse!"

Cast, backstage, friends and admirers surged rowdily into the tavern. Bill Wood penciled in his diary: "Willy Warren's Pierre dropped like a stone. He killed the part, but Willy has probably laid a ghost."

* * * * *

Second-generation politicians, none old enough to remember colonial rule, inspired by nationalist fervor and hatred of their former overlords, who had successfully blockaded their shipping, had had enough. No word had been received that the government of England intended to heed the advice of the English merchants that the orders in council be revoked to avert a crisis. Popular resentment against Britain had spread like a bush fire as war-hawks called for unity in speech after speech, but not until war against Britain was actually declared on June 20, 1812, did Philadelphia's theatre world sit up and take note.

"Oh, not another war with England!" Maria exclaimed. "Well, I'm seriously thinking of seeking an annulment of my marriage. I'll renounce dowry but keep my title. That's the price of my love for John. He's not coming back to me."

"Oh, Maria, I'm so glad you've decided this way. Jock Murray's sweet on you. You can remarry any day, have lots of children," said Fanny.

Maria chuckled. "A doctor's wife? No, thank you. I just want to be free, but this war's going to close the theatres. That appalls me. They've done it before as in the Revolutionary War. They outlawed exhibitions of shows, plays, and other diversions. People seen acting or attending plays lost their jobs. At any rate, The Smugglers Players will be hit. Georgetown's waterways will be seething with gunboats, the Convivial Club interested only in naval battles, pirates and their shipping."

"Philadelphia will go on flourishing," Fanny dismissed Maria's gloom.

"You heard Bill Wood's engaged to one of the Westray girls," Maria would not be stopped. "Juliana. New York is billing her a star. Bringing her to the Chestnut will be a cinch. Bill will cast her in all the lead roles. These actor-managers are a pest. It'll be the Ann Merry story all over again."

"No one can eclipse you, darling," said Fanny. "Not after your brilliant Belvidera, and Willy Warren and Bill Wood have got to look sharp. The Chestnut's got competition."

"What? You really believe the new Walnut Street Theatre can compete with old Chestnut? Why the Walnut's only just opened as a playhouse."

"The rivalry's already intense. Willy's installing gaslight. He thinks the novelty will outdo the New York theatres. Anyhow, if you're closing down The Smugglers till after the war it'll not be so hard for me going back to New York, quitting the stage to look after Pa," said Fanny.

Maria hesitated, shot an anxious glance at Fanny with her large bright eyes in a pale face beneath the still beautiful crown of auburn hair. "You'll never quit Fanny," she said fondly. "Remember Bella? Being stage-struck is like a drug that hooks you."

• • • • •

When Maria received Joseph's letter, Gampy had been dead sometime. River traffic was congested with war vessels and stagecoaches, bringing mail to a standstill by gullied and potholed earth roads as storm rains fell with nerve-shattering ferocity. Fanny had already left Philadelphia for New York after a stupendous sendoff by the troupe and the Chestnut had been temporarily taken over by bullying engineers putting in gaslights. But there was plenty of noise in the taverns, actors and actresses taking advantage of the lull, Bill Wood was casting around for ideas for next season's productions. He was favoring opening with James Barker's *America*, calling it a one act masque in poetic dialogue. "Exalts the nation's genius," he said recalling the Chestnut's success with *Tears and Smiles* a few years back before Maria's time. She borrowed a copy, discovered it to be a comedy of manners, and settled down to enjoy it when a courier arrived with Joseph's letter.

She stared at the stained and mud-spattered envelope not daring to open it, overwhelmed by a sudden premonition of disaster. "Not Gampy!" she cried in shock when she nerved herself to do so. "Oh no! God knows how they will get over this!" And she wept, heartbroken, over the pages of James Barker's *Tears*.

· · · · ·

At The Oaks, dinner was laid for one. Theodosia had not left her boudoir these past months. No member of the family or close friend was present to greet Joseph arriving from the state capital. Today, he was elected governor. Today, he had achieved the accolade for which he had fought so hard and so long. But he had no appetite and dejectedly watched his Negroes serve up dishes, and remove them hardly touched, with white-gloved hands and lowered eyes.

Had there been anyone to share his table, it would have made no difference. All he wanted was for Theodosia, restored in mind and body, to celebrate. He did not take his usual cigar and glass of port. Leaving the dining hall, he slowly mounted the broad stairway, delaying his approach to Theodosia's boudoir, dreading what he might find. Suddenly the Negress in attendance came out, stepped back with a gasp and called "'Tis de Maussa" as Joseph swept past her into the room.

Theodosia met him, strangely invigorated. "We are leaving for Richmond Hill," she told him. "I do not know why I am here. Father will be anxious. I always do the flowers when we have guests."

"Theodosia, my dearest wife," he stammered. "This is your home with me, your husband Joseph."

Theodosia prattled on unhearing. "I want to go home to Richmond Hill," she pleaded like a lost child.

"When you are better, my dear," Joseph placated her taking her hands in his. "When you have regained your strength. I promise!"

It was no use. He could not tell her tonight that he had been elected governor, let alone remind her that Richmond Hill was no more. He felt utterly helpless and rang for the Negress who alone could comfort his adored

Yankee wife whom he had brought with such pride to the Waccamaw only twelve years ago.

· · · · ·

The coincidence of Joseph's election as governor of South Carolina in time of war invested him with a power not normally accorded to governors. He was doubly declared the Honorable Joseph Alston, Governor and Commander-in-Chief, in and over the state. Theodosia was too frail to attend the impressive ceremony on the portico of the state house in Columbia. With his dearest ambition fulfilled, he sat alone in an agony of despair over the loss of their son and of Theodosia's illness.

When he returned home, he was enraged to find a physician sent by his father-in-law to take his beloved wife away from him. "Timothy Green is an old friend," he read in Aaron Burr's message.

"My wife is too sick to travel," he faced Green determinedly. "I forbid the journey!"

"I have already examined your wife," Green replied, "and it is my professional opinion that she must be taken to her father without delay. It is the only hope for her recovery."

Joseph flung himself down in a chair, his head in his hands. Timothy Green stood staring out of the window. The rice fields lay bare, the cool season at its height.

To lose Theodosia, for her to follow Gampy to the grave, was too much for Joseph to contemplate. He rose and turned to Green with a final desperate protest. "She is too sick to attempt the journey overland."

"With that I am in agreement," Green replied. "A passage is available for us on the *Patriot*."

Joseph had no more words left. "What kind of vessel is the *Patriot*?"

"A pilot boat. It's been out privateering, but she is now returning to New York with her guns under deck."

"When does she sail?" Joseph asked anxiously.

"On Old Year's Night."

"So soon?" Joseph said in dismay.

"Her sailing master is an experienced seaman, a New Yorker. Captain Overstocks," Green reassured Joseph.

"Nevertheless I will write a safe-conduct for my dear wife in case Overstocks should encounter warring British vessels," Joseph said. "And now I wish you goodnight!"

· · · · ·

Three weeks went by with no word from the vessel despite the *Patriot*'s reputation for speed.

What had happened to those aboard? There was still no word, only rumors that there had been a heavy gale off North Carolina's Cape Fear on Old Year's Night.

♦ ♦ ♦ ♦ ♦

The South Carolina coast had not been struck by a hurricane of such ferocity in sixty years. Terrifying walls of water bore down upon the shore, swallowing up vessels, smashing summer houses on the islands, while hurricane-force gales tore through the streets of Georgetown ripping off roofs, blowing in windows, and flattening the standing rice crop. The screams of the terrified communities up and down the coast were lost in the thunder of the winds. Many dead were found floating among the wreckage, white and Negro together, as the storm began to abate.

Only recently, Judge Bay's ruling had provided no penalty for disobeying orders to defend the state, overturning Joseph's imposition of a general court-martial upon forty deserting captains of the militia. Harassed victims of the storm swung overnight to Joseph's conviction that anarchy within the militia had to be arrested and belatedly, the legislature brought the state militia under the same regulations as federal troops ordering an immediate cleanup in the wake of the terrible natural disaster.

Leaving the captains to the task, the forty still resentful at the election of a politician as their commander-in-chief, Joseph retreated to The Castle. The hurricane had battered his plantation and The Oaks filled him with melancholy. But The Castle on Debordieu, once the derision of neighboring planters, had alone survived the hurricane on the beaches.

He stood on the verandah as he had done time and time again in the past few months, its stilts facing the ocean and relentlessly, his obsession with Theodosia's fate returned.

Chapter Thirty-Five

The wretched war with England straggled Joseph's tenure as state governor, a cruel, wanton, and senseless war inflaming feelings against Britain for the second time.

Joseph, caught in the war policy of his southern Democrat compatriots to whom revenge was everything, retired to The Oaks at the end of it, a much abused, embittered, and lonely man.

Frantically, he had appointed team after team of investigators to unravel the mystery surrounding the missing *Patriot*, but there was nothing. He had come to accept that he would never know the fate of his beloved Theodosia, and now he simply lost the will to live.

But for his devoted sister, Maria, the Philadelphia Chestnut continued to flourish with her playing leading roles. Bill Wood's management classed him among the hustlers, the "dollar grabbers", his actors and actresses giving fine performances to audiences relishing every spectacular melodrama. War and confusion had no part in Bill Wood's repertoire. The times were exciting. He was exciting, optimistic, boastful, getting twice the work out of the company than his partner Willy Warren who affectionately nicknamed the theatre "Old Drury" to confound the war-hawks. Maria was on top of the world, until one day just as she was going on stage.

• • • • •

For an instant there was a touch of hysteria in Maria's laughter, but Piers stayed cool. Then she laughed again because it eased her tension, for she was striking an attitude of shattered relations forever. "Marry Fanny?" she tossed her head back. Her eyes bright.

"Oh, butterfly! You never really loved me. Fanny and I have found a common cause. We have the same roots. We can make each other happy."

"Common cause? Same roots? What do you mean?" said Maria sharply.

"Fanny has quit the stage, and has joined the campaign for the abolition of southern slavery," Piers said.

"A philanthropist, eh?" Maria said bitingly. "But foreign slave trade was abolished ten years ago."

"Yes, but not domestic slavery. I've become a Yankee sympathizer, too," Piers said apologetically. "Don't you see Maria?"

"Of course I see," Maria said angrily. "They've a saying in the theatre about the desire for freedom. The Yankee from the English, the Indian from the Yankees, and the Negro from his bondage. Half the melodramas caricature aspects of it. But Yankees distributing inflammatory pamphlets on the streets of New York about southern slavery, it's presumptuous! You of all people, Piers. You could hardly tear yourself away from Fairfield. They'll be inciting civil war next!"

Piers laughed lightly. "It'll never come to that Butterfly. We're all too busy adopting an anti-foreign attitude, building a new country. You will come to our wedding?" he appealed.

"You think I would let Fanny down? Never! Of course I'll be there. But Piers, whatever happens..." Maria veered from anger to meekness.

"We are bound to one another forever by our past," Piers finished. "Freedom is nothing but a myth!"

"It's what we all want."

"The New Yorkers are even calling this last bloody war the second War of Independence. Nationalism is a hot potato. We're dramatizing every battle. The Park's got Grice's *Battle of New Orleans* running at present. Audiences are crazy about it. Celebrates the heroic defense of the town by gangs of backwoodsmen putting to rout British infantry raiding from the sea. Oh, I almost forgot. Thought you'd want to see this," Piers dived into his breast pocket. "I cut it from the *New York Evening Post* just as I was leaving for Philadelphia."

• • • • •

Tears of emotion rolled down Maria's cheeks. Never in her wildest dreams could she have imagined herself attracting the attention of the greatest actress on the English stage.

"Dry up, girl!" said Bill Wood. "I'd give anything to be invited to make my début on the London stage."

"I'm ecstatic, Bill! A chance to meet the wonderful Sarah Siddons!"

"Ah! Beware that tempestuous woman," Bill said, beating the air with a grandiose sweep of his hand. "Rising seventy and she will act you right off the stage with extravagant gestures and strike terror in you with that resonant voice."

"Only, I hate the sea. I think I'm more afraid of the horrendous Atlantic crossing."

"Pooh! Tragedy airs! Hundreds have done it before you and you owe it to Willy Dunlap. He set you up in your acting career. Poor old Dunlap's run into debt. One of our greatest giants hiding away in some dingy hole writing a history of our turbulent American theatre. For myself, I say the gods of the theatre are English still."

"I could have crossed the Atlantic once," said Maria reflectively. "When I was a young bride of nineteen. I was carrying my child and let my husband travel alone. Siddons was playing her famous roles at Drury Lane."

"What a missed opportunity!"

"I've told myself that a thousand times. I'm thirty-eight now, and free."

"Go then. Go!"

But, there was something Maria had to do first on this side of the Atlantic. She boarded the mail coach for the tortuous overland journey south.

♦ ♦ ♦ ♦ ♦

"Joseph is dead," Algie said

"I am too late!" said Maria.

"The Oaks is mine now. Why have you come?"

"I came with news for Joseph," Maria said as she handed Algie the press cutting.

"A confession by one of the piratical crew that captured the *Patriot*?" Algie read. "So Theodosia was made to walk the plank! It was murder then. Joseph would never have got over it."

"Better than never knowing. I've seen Joseph's obituary. 'A man of courage in times of adversity,' it said. I shall never get over losing Joseph. I think the family should do something really magnanimous to keep his memory alive."

"Such as what, Maria?"

"I've been thinking, why not manumit Joseph's slaves?"

"You must be mad!" Algie shouted.

"Joseph fought passionately for the prohibition of slaves from entering the state," Maria argued. "It would be a fitting tribute."

"You've been away too long Maria. You're out of touch. We'll secede from the Union first!"

"Oh Algie! You always were father's son."

"Our roots are here," Algie said impatiently. "Our family burial ground. Joseph's tomb."

Maria sighed. "With his beloved child now, and my Johnny, and Grandpa Joseph, we are clinging to a rope of sand, Algie."

"Grandpa Joseph was wrong," said Algie.

"He loved Joseph. Father was wrong. He never accepted Joseph." Maria said as she walked over to her mare, took the bridle in her hand ready to leave. Before mounting she gazed wistfully at the long vista of rice plats in their golden glory. Suddenly, she went rigid gripped by fear. A throng of shadowy figures rose over the fluttering heads of grain, petrifying apparitions with outstretched arms and beckoning fingers. "Look!" she cried.

"I can see nothing," said Algie following her gaze.

In mute distress Maria swung into the saddle and galloped helter-skelter down the avenue of live oaks out on to the King's Highway putting distance between herself and Grandpa Joseph's legacy of ghosts.